Kitty Valentine
dates a Billionaire

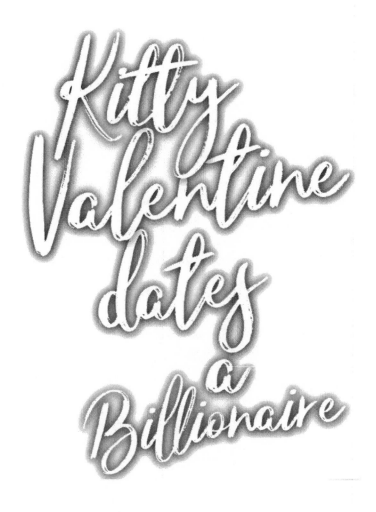

JILLIAN DODD

Editor: Jovana Shirley, Unforeseen Editing,
www.unforseenediting.com

Jillian Dodd Inc. Madeira Beach, FL

Jillian Dodd, The Keatyn Chronicles, and Spy Girl are Registered
Trademarks of Jillian Dodd Inc.

ISBN: 978-1-946793-30-0

Books by Jillian Dodd

Chapter One

THE THING ABOUT being a best-selling romance author is how everybody thinks your life is nothing but one big romcom. Or a nasty, filthy erotic story.

My life is neither of those things. Why? Because I'm a best-selling author—obviously—and therefore, I have no time for anything but writing. It's sort of an ugly cycle.

Don't start feeling sorry for me anytime soon though. I do make an attempt every so often to venture from my Upper West Side apartment and pretend to be an actual human being. You'll see us sometimes—the writers who occasionally venture from their caves, squinting up at the sun like they've never seen it before and asking a random passerby what year it is.

Like at this very moment, as I line my blue eyes and apply a little mascara in preparation for a rare daytime excursion. I then pull my long brown hair into a sleek bun at the nape of my neck. Nothing fancy. This isn't a date or a release party or anything like that.

When was the last time I put on makeup and did

anything with my hair? Last Thursday maybe? No, Wednesday—when I met up with my best friend, Hayley, to celebrate her promotion. Before that? It's a mystery wrapped up in a pair of yoga pants.

Once again, don't get the wrong idea. I don't need an internet fundraiser set up in my name—besides, you can't create a fundraiser to get somebody a life. And I'm not deliberately a recluse. I'm fine when it comes to self-confidence, and I do enjoy the feeling of sunshine on my skin every once in a while.

But writing, especially one or two books a year, means a lot of time spent with my butt in my chair and my fingers on the keyboard.

Life as Kitty Valentine is an interesting balancing act between living up to my last name—honestly, with a name like Valentine, what else was I supposed to do with my life?—and living like a normal human person. Today, I'm doing regular human things because it's time for me and my agent to meet up with my editor in her office.

This is an important day, which means I'm breaking out a new dress I purchased on a late-night shopping binge. A girl's gotta do something with her evenings. By the time I lift my head from behind my laptop screen, it's too late to visit a store. They tend to close at reasonable times. The navy-blue sheath fits me like a glove, just like the slingback pumps I bought during the same shopping session.

My latest book, *Candy-Coated Love*, released recently. It's a heartwarming story about a couple who meet in their apartment building when his golden retriever jumps on her. I always meet with my team to celebrate hitting the *New York Times* Best Sellers list. My agent, Lois, gets an advance copy of the list, and while she could easily email it to me, she likes to maintain our special tradition.

Though she hardly looks like she's in a special sort of mood when she meets me in the publisher's lobby after a brief cab ride.

Everything okay?" I ask with a smile, which she doesn't return.

Granted, she's had enough work done on her seventy-year-old face to make smiling a difficulty, but I don't even get the permanent smirk her mouth seems to have settled into. More like a scowl.

"How's the next book coming?" she replies.

Yeah, that's the Lois I know and wish I could love. This is pretty much the extent of our relationship. I write; she sells. There are no flowers or rainbows.

But that's okay. I get enough flowers and rainbows in the books I write. Besides, she's a force to be reckoned with in the publishing industry. I know how lucky I am to have her in my corner.

My editor isn't in there when her assistant escorts us to her office, so we have to wait. And wait.

And then, just to keep things interesting ... we wait.

I'm starting to get nervous. That nervous energy propels me out of my cushioned chair positioned in front of Maggie's desk. There are fantastic views of the city from this high up, and I decide to take a look out there. As I progress across the room, the framed articles hanging on the wall catch my attention.

Because they're about me. Wouldn't you be distracted by articles written about you?

Phenom writer hits number one NYT Best Sellers list with debut novel, Sweet Love. The wholesome romance about falling in love over coffee and puppies flies off bookshelves …

Only twenty-one and fresh out of college when she wrote the story that was originally Harry Potter fan fiction …

Kitty Valentine is the hottest name in romance …

There are other articles, tons of them, charting a stellar career. My first four books debuted at number one on the list. What can I say? I'm blessed, not only with good ideas and the ability to write them down, but also with an editor and agent capable of putting my work out into the world in a big way.

Maggie rushes into the office, making me jump in surprise as her heels click against the floor. My smile is wide, my arms lifting for a hug by the time she reaches me. This is our usual routine. Smiles, hugs, congratulations all around.

Routine doesn't seem to be what Maggie's in the mood for today. She rushes right past me with barely a glance and sits behind her desk. "Take a seat," she invites, gesturing to the chair I just left.

Oh. This is new. Why are my knees knocking a little as I sit down? It's just that, book after book, we've done the same thing. Heck, she didn't even bring in any champagne. A cheap bottle of wine would've been acceptable. I'm not a snob.

"Ladies, we have a problem," she says, looking from Lois to me and staying there.

"What?" I ask with my heart in my throat.

"You didn't hit the list this week. The book is a bomb."

Maggie has always been good at getting to the heart of the matter with little fanfare, but her abruptness is still a shocker.

"It didn't? It is?" *Look at me, the fancy writer, knowing so many words.*

She shrugs her thin shoulders. "Sweet romance isn't selling anymore. You're going to have to write something on-trend."

I look to Lois, whose very stiff face hasn't loosened up any. "Do you have any idea what that means, agent of mine?" I whisper.

Maggie doesn't give her the chance to explain, jumping in to do it herself. "The current tropes that are selling the best, I mean. The trends. You can't tell me you don't keep up with what the rest of the industry is doing."

I could just about melt into my chair, and my face is about as red as my lipstick. I can feel it burning, like eggs-cooking-on-the-sidewalk levels of heat. "I don't exactly have a lot of extra time on my hands with the pace I have to keep up," I point out, but even to my ears, it sounds like a lame excuse.

She lets it go, charitable for the first time since she came in. "*Her Stepbrother's Baby. Balls Deep. His Wolf Highness.* Those are a few titles that are selling well right now. MC clubs are still hot too."

Those are the titles? "What's an MC club?"

She blinks hard. "Motorcycle club. How men with tattoos who live filthy, dangerous lives, love fiercely, and are finally tamed by the only women strong enough to take them on." Her eyes have a strange light that matches the tone of her voice. *Is it excitement?* "If that doesn't turn you on, what about bears or beasts that transform into humans?"

It's my turn to blink. "Like, sex with a hippogriff?"

"Everything isn't Harry Potter fanfic, Kitty," she sighs, making me blush again. "Shifters. Breeders."

"Breeders?" Do I even want to know?

"When a woman is forced to have someone's baby."

What an education today is turning out to be.

"And women like this?" I ask, scrunching up my face.

Somewhere along the way, the romance world I

6

know and love has turned into something I hardly recognize. I wouldn't be able to put the books Maggie's describing on the same shelf as the novels my mom used to read, the books that got me into romance in the first place. My books would be scandalized. I'd have to turn them around, so the covers didn't face each other.

"Kitty," Maggie says, "a single kiss isn't doing it for romance readers anymore. In your last book, the heroine didn't even give the guy head. No anal. Not even a well-placed thumb."

"I think that's off-limits for most self-respecting women," I reply. "Butt stuff, I mean."

"No sex toys either," she adds.

"Furry handcuffs, once!"

She rolls her eyes. "Come on. It was in a flash-back scene from a seventh-grade Halloween party and didn't involve sex in any way. You know what readers want? For the hero to cuff the heroine to the bed and screw the living shit out of her."

"Maggie!" I gasp.

She's never spoken this way to me before.

"That's how it is." She shrugs, leaning back in her leather chair. "Women want to be treated like dirty whores in the bedroom. They love foul-mouthed, alpha males. You write sweet betas."

"Uh, the real meaning of beta is …" I begin.

It doesn't matter. She bolts up from her chair, pacing in front of the window. Her heels click smartly again, her rapid pace keeping time with the beat of my heart.

"When's the last time you got laid?"

"I don't see what that has to do with anything."

"That long, huh?"

It's like I've stepped into a bizarro world. *Since when do we get so personal?* "What's that got to do with it?" I insist, folding my arms.

"Your characters, when they finally do it, are in the missionary position. Always. In fact, your books are like the missionary position. They get the job done, but that's about it." She pulls a single printout from a folder on her desk and drops it into my lap. "See for yourself. The sales figures for your latest book. Unlike the women you write, they suck."

"I write missionary position because the man is on top and in control," I point out. Okay, so it's lame, but I have to redeem myself somehow.

Lois is no help. When I look over at her, hoping she'll back me up, I find she's nodded off.

Maggie shakes her head at me. "Women want hot, messy sex. Dirty sex with a foul-mouthed, hot-as-hell, take-what-he-wants guy who'll leave them breathless. And he needs to have some kind of secret past only the heroine can heal him from."

"With her vagina?" I ask, raising a skeptical eyebrow.

"Exactly." She smiles, like I was asking a serious question.

"Don't women want to be treated with respect?" I can't help but ask. "Wouldn't she do better to get him into counseling? I can't write books where women are treated poorly."

"How is being given a good fucking being treated poorly?" she challenges, perching on the edge of her desk and staring straight at me.

I have no response to this, and she can tell. I know it because the look on her face turns to one of smug triumph.

"Listen, sweetheart, it's up to you. You can stick to your morals and write the sweet, bland love stories you write now—which you'll have to self-publish—or you can write something hot, which we'll publish."

She leans in, eyes narrowing. "We can't buy the novel you're currently working on. We can't afford to. I'm sorry, kiddo. I wish this were better news. But that's the state of the business nowadays. Write to please yourself, or write to the market. It's your choice."

My choice. It's like being asked if I'd rather die via firing squad or hanging. It isn't really a choice at all.

If I plan on making an income and continuing to write, which is the only thing I've ever wanted to do with my life, I'd better start learning how to be dirty—or at least, to write characters capable of doing very dirty things.

Even if I can't imagine doing any of them myself.

She keeps talking, but I can barely hear any of it over the pounding of my heart and the sinking of my stomach.

So much for being the hottest name in romance.

Chapter Two

MY EDITOR WAS very clear. No more sappy love stories.

So, I do what any self-respecting author would do in the face of sacrificing their morals and integrity for the sake of maintaining a career: I go to the liquor store. After all, there's no way I'm going to be able to write the sort of things she described while sober. I can hardly even think about it without blushing.

I've heard the saying, *Write drunk, edit sober*, before and never understood the reasoning behind it until now. Indeed, today has been an education.

By the time I get home to my walk-up, I'm struggling to make it up the stairs with a grocery sack full of booze. Anybody who saw me would probably imagine I was having a party—and if they knew the truth, they'd probably wonder how to stage an intervention.

Suddenly, as I'm a few stairs away from my floor, a golden retriever comes barreling down the hall in my direction.

"Phoebe, don't jump," a deep, rich voice chides.

A voice belonging to the drop-dead gorgeous man who shares the floor with me, his apartment sitting across from mine.

Okay, so maybe I took ideas from my own real life and used them for my last bomb of a book. Right down to the breed of dog involved. A girl can only be so imaginative.

Which is a shame because I'm going to have to start using my imagination in ways I never thought possible.

A six-foot-plus mountain of lean muscle comes trotting down the hall after the dog, a perfect smile lighting up his face. My beautiful neighbor, a guy handsome enough to make me a little sweaty at the very sight of him.

Is it crazy that in the year we've lived across the hall from each other, we've never spoken outside a passing hello? Considering how perfect he is—like a fairy-tale prince, right down to the adorable, playful dog—maybe I need to get my head examined.

He's gentle when he pulls the dog away from me. "Sit," he orders.

When she does, gazing up at him with huge dark brown eyes that practically scream adoration, he pats her on the head. I have to bite my tongue to keep from asking if there's anything I can do to get a pat on the head like that. A girl can dream, right? That doesn't mean she has to make a fool of herself.

"Thanks." I manage to laugh a little, feeling breathless in the light of that smile of his.

Boy, it's not even fair for a man to be this hand-some.

His dark eyes look me up and down, and he must like what he sees since his smile widens.

He then notices the bag just about spilling out from under my arm. "You need some help with that?" he asks before taking it from me.

Wow, this is going well. It's one of those perfect meet-cutes, right?

Except for the general disarray in my apartment. I've been working hard on that little book my editor won't buy, which means pretty much everything else in the world has fallen by the wayside. Including picking up my dirty laundry from the general vicinity of the hamper and tossing out empty takeout containers.

Mom always said sloppiness would be the death of me. I doubt she had this exact situation in mind though.

Also, a bag bulging with liquor bottles isn't usually a standard meet-cute accessory.

"You know what? I think I'm okay." Once I have the front door unlocked, I spin in place and take the bag back. "But thank you."

He takes this mini rejection well, turning his attention to the contents of the bag. There go my cheeks, flushing hotter than ever.

"Having a party?" he asks, still good-natured.

"Sure am. A party of one." I somehow manage to smile in the face of my disappointment.

He doesn't need to know the sordid details of my depressing life. Though I guess when a person buys this much liquor all at once and admits they're the only one drinking it, the message comes through.

"Well, I'm Matt. It's a shame it took this long for us to introduce ourselves." He thrusts out his hand for a shake. "But I'm glad we finally had the chance."

"Me too. And I'm Kitty." It's not easy to keep from giggling when those eyes of his are locked on mine, and my hand is in his much larger, much stronger one.

He's going to have a truly wonderful idea of me once this is all over, isn't he? It'll be another year before he dares to talk to me again.

Again, he eyes the liquor. "You can't drink that all alone, you know."

"No?"

"No. You'll die. And in a few days, you'll start to stink. And I'll have to go in with the police to identify your body, and is that how you want me to remember you? In your bed?"

Gulp. Yes, in fact, I would like him to remember me in bed. Preferably above me with the muscles of his shoulders flexing and bunching as he holds himself up. Or when he reaches down to stroke my cheek, to kiss me for the thousandth time.

"Naked?" I blurt out.

His eyes go wide. "Pardon?"

"Would I be naked in this scenario?"

"Uh, I think the bigger problem here is you being dead. Naked or otherwise."

"I'll have to remember to keep my clothes on
then."

He's smiling again, though maybe it's because
he feels sorry for me and wonders if it's safe for me
to live alone.

"Or you could not drink too much at once. Seriously, I'd hate to have to identify your body, no
matter how much you've got on."

I can't decide if he's making fun of me, flirting
with me, being neighborly, or feeling legitimately
concerned that I might be the sort of person who'd
drink all this alcohol at once.

"Thanks. I won't," I mutter, reaching behind me
to turn the knob and backing up just far enough to
get into the apartment so he won't see anything that
might embarrass me. I've embarrassed myself
enough. "See ya."

I then lean against the closed door with a sigh.
I'm such an idiot. He was bound to find out
sometime.

That's enough of that for today anyway. I have
much bigger fish to fry than the matter of the hottie
from across the hall. Such as how I'm supposed to
write a really filthy, on-trend romance.

Which means taking the liquor to the kitchen
and deciding who to start the party with. "Will it be
you, Mr. Jack Daniel's?" I ask, tapping the top of the

bottle with my nails. "Or you, Mr. Stoli? Ooh, Mr. Patrón. We haven't gotten together in far too long."

Tequila it is.

After a single shot, I get the heck out of my fancy work clothes and into my regular work clothes— a T-shirt, plaid pajama pants, and fuzzy slippers. After a second shot, I'm feeling slightly better about this business of dirty-writing. *It can't be that hard, can it? I've written best-sellers, for Pete's sake. I can do this.*

So, I go to my office, which would be the bedroom just off the living room if I had a roommate. The apartment isn't anywhere near huge, but it's perfect for me—and it's close enough to Central Park that I can take a walk there when I'm good and stuck in my work.

I'm not stuck now, sitting behind my laptop and cracking my knuckles. Mind over matter. It's all about attitude. I'll start with a sexy scene to get the juices flowing … so to speak.

Funny thing, but the notion of dirty sex is easier to manage so soon after talking with Matt. Maybe not so funny. Maybe I need to do more talking with him if the mere sight of his gorgeous face and body is enough to get me thinking along these lines.

He caressed the petals of her silky folds.

I type roughly half a page into the scene before he moves on top of her, sinking his …

"Oh no," I groan, rolling my eyes at myself.

Missionary again.

I must not have drunk enough.

I take the laptop to the kitchen and pour another shot. There's gotta be a way to do this that'll be better for my liver, but desperate times call for desperate measures. And I'm desperate.

By the time I take the fourth shot, I'm ready to go again. Only here's the problem—well, two problems.

For one thing, I just drank four shots, and they're starting to hit me.

For the other thing, missionary sex is just where my mind goes. *Have I honestly only ever had sex in that one single position?* I think back with a frown. Twenty-five years old, and I can only remember doing it that way—and once when we were both on our sides. So, two positions.

No, three! I hold up a fist in triumph.

There was that one time in college where he was behind me. Yeah, that's something to be proud of.

What I don't need is alcohol. What I need is research.

Short of having a guy handcuffed to my bed, there's not much I can do besides ask the closest man in the vicinity. Which means taking one more shot for courage then darting across the hall before I can talk myself out of it.

My knock inspires a fresh round of frantic barking, and I cringe in preparation for a golden retriever attack. Except Phoebe doesn't come charging when the door opens. In fact, her barking and scratching at the door are quickly replaced by a softer whining noise.

When the door opens, my jaw hits the floor. At least, that's how it feels. Mr. Matt is now shirtless, a little out of breath, and just a bit sweaty, like he was in the middle of a workout. It takes real effort on my part not to think about the sort of workout I'd like to give him, especially when my eyes are naturally led down, down his defined chest and abs to the delicious, sharp V of muscle leading into his pants.

Hot. Damn.

If he notices my ogling, he has the decency not to call me on it. "Sorry it took me a minute to answer." He grins. "I had to put Phoebe in her kennel, so she wouldn't jump on you. What's up?"

What's up? I can hardly remember why I came over here. "Uh ... oh, right. What's your favorite position?"

"My favorite ..." he mutters with a frown. "Are we talking politics? Or sex?"

"Sex." *Please say missionary. Please prove me right.*

"Hmm." He's trying to look serious, but it's not working. "I'd have to show you."

Now's not the time to be sexy and adorable, particularly when I'm drunk and feeling vulnerable to his charm. "Please, tell me. This is important research."

"Research? In that case ..." He taps a finger to

his lips, smirking, and turns his eyes up toward the ceiling. "If I absolutely had to choose to only have sex in one position for the rest of my life, it would be reverse cowgirl."

"Really?" It's not easy, trying to look serious and professional at a time like this. "That's fascinating."

"Indeed." He lowers his hands, placing them sideways in front of his hips like he's holding on to something. Or someone. "I'm a butt man; what can I say? I like watching it bounce up and down when she's riding me."

Jeez Louise. My mouth is suddenly bone dry. "Uh." That's all I manage to say. And I'm a writer.

He shrugs. "What exactly is this research for, if you don't mind me asking?"

Rather than come up with an answer—like, the truth for instance—my good friend Patrón gives me an idea. "You're a nice-looking guy. I bet you have a lot of sex. With all the girls you bring home on the nights you don't get in until four in the morning."

He's not smiling anymore. "You know when I come home?" he asks, taking a backward step to put more space between himself and the serial killer from across the hall, who's been studying his habits. At least, that's how I'd feel in his shoes.

"You didn't answer my question."

"Do you go out much?"

"I'm the one asking questions right now," I remind him, shaking a finger in his face. He's starting to go a little blurry, truth be told. "And if you need to know, I work late at night. I'm usually awake until all hours."

"What do you do?"

"I'm a writer." Right, and I'm holding my laptop to prove it. I thrust it his way. "Ta-da."

Of course, I sort of forgot what I was writing before I made this little trek across the hall. This might not have been the best time to present my work.

It's too late though since he has already taken the computer from me and is now reading. Aloud. *"He caressed the petals of her silky folds?* What do you write about? Flowers?"

"No. Romance. How would you say that in a dirty way?"

"It depends on what it means. What silky folds?"

I roll my eyes. "Down there," I whisper, pointing. "Her vagina."

His mouth twitches like he's trying to hold back a laugh. "Oh. I see. If you write romance, don't you know how to dirty it up on your own?"

I have to sigh. I've been holding that sigh back all day, ever since the meeting with Maggie, and it feels good to let it out. "No. My books are sweet and wholesome. They focus on relationships, not on gratuitous sex. Think lovemaking instead. Only that's not what's selling right now, which is why I'm drinking. I need to get myself loosened up, so I can write what my editor wants to read. I have to learn how to write dirty sex."

"Now, it's all coming together—no pun intended." He winks.

I'm a little too tipsy to figure out what that's supposed to mean, so I only smile. "Right. So, what do I say? *He shoved his big, hardened sex*—no, *manhood*. No, *his dick*. Hmm. *He shoved his big, hard dick*?"

He winces, wrinkling his nose like he just smelled something putrid. "Why don't you say, *He shoved his big, hard cock*?"

"Yes!" I squeal, clapping like mad. "This is the help I need! *He shoved his big, hard cock into her ...* um ... *silky, moist ...* no. No, that's not good. *Her silky vagina that was all ...* wait! I know! *Juicy for him*. Huh?" I ask, feeling pretty proud.

Until his nose wrinkles again, that is.

"No offense, but that's awful. Moist? Silky? How about, *He shoved his hard cock into her sweet, wet pussy*?"

Gulp. *Is it just the tequila, or is he not joking anymore?* "That's perfect," I whisper. "Thanks. I'll be going home now." Except when I try to grab for the laptop, I can't figure out which of the three in front of me to reach for. "I'm dizzy."

The last thing I remember is falling into a pair of strong arms.

Chapter Three

THE SUN IS rude.

That's the first thought to bubble to the surface of my dehydrated, hungover brain on waking up. *How dare the sun shine in my face this way.* Well, the sun was all the way on the other side of the world when I drank too much. It doesn't know any better than to rudely awaken me.

Drank too much.

This isn't my bed. The sheets are way too fancy.

What happened?

I have to pry open one eye to look around, sun or no sun. *What did I do last night?*

The sight of a naked shoulder next to me is enough to inspire a screech of surprise and horror.

Which inspires a dog to start barking, which inspires my head to pound harder than it already was.

The shoulder flexes, moves, and suddenly, the person beside me is rolling over to give me a smile. I know that smile. *Oh crap.*

"How are you feeling?" Matt asks with a knowing look.

"Um … I'm not sure." Because clearly, he doesn't want the laundry list of everything running through my head. *How did I end up in bed with him? Did we do it? If so, how could I possibly forget having sex with this beautiful man?*

Then again, it's all a blank after a certain point. My memory's a total wash.

"You were kind of messed up last night," he explains, sympathetic. "You passed out in my arms actually."

Okay, so that pretty much makes me want to die of embarrassment. "What then?" I ask in barely a whisper. I'm not even sure I want to know.

"And then I laid you down on my couch, out in the living room. I made sure you were still breathing okay. No offense, but I couldn't stop thinking about that bag of liquor bottles from yesterday. I was afraid you might really have alcohol poisoning. I almost took you to the hospital. But you finally came to and said you only had four or maybe five shots of tequila. Painful, but it didn't seem like that would kill you."

"So, how did I end up in your bed?" I can't believe I have to ask this, but that's what happens when a girl who doesn't normally drink that much at once just so happened to forget to eat anything beforehand. I don't think I've ever been so humiliated.

Oh, wait, things can always get worse.

I sit up, facing away from Matt because I'm too

embarrassed to look at him, and throw back the blankets. The cool morning air hits my skin. All of my skin. Like, my entire body.

"I'm naked!" I shriek, covering myself up again. "Oh my God! Did we—"

"No!" Matt laughs, and for a second there, I'm wondering if he finds the idea of sexing me truly hilarious. He's certainly laughing hard enough. "No, you stripped your clothes off. Actually, you got partway—your pants—before you fell down and threw up all over yourself."

"I did not."

"You did. And on my rug. Anyway, you wanted to get into bed, and I figured that was safer than letting you fall down again and actually hurting yourself. Only I wasn't about to let you get into bed with puke on your clothes. Don't worry," he adds when I just about faint. "I was a good boy and didn't peek. Notice how bundled up you were. We weren't even sharing a blanket."

He's right about that. I was pretty much a burrito in my blanket while he's still covered in another one. That bodes well.

Even so, I have no choice but to put my hand over my face and shake my head. I can barely take a peek at him from between my fingers.

Though I do take a peek, and what I see almost makes me forget how bad my head feels and how I wish I hadn't had so much to drink. I dated in college, but they were just boys.

Matt? He's all man. His brown hair's a little mussed. His cheeks are covered in scruff that only makes him harder to resist. His eyes, I notice, aren't brown like I thought they were. They're hazel, and in my writer's mind, I imagine them changing color depending on the light and what he's wearing.

Has a man ever looked better in the morning? Especially shirtless, which definitely works in his favor.

It only makes me feel worse, to be honest. "I'm so embarrassed."

He's got it all together, and he looks great while I'm the messy chick from across the hall who threw up all over his apartment.

"You don't have to be. This sort of thing happens. If anything, I'm glad we hung out, and I finally know what you do for a living. I've gotta be honest. I thought you were either a flight attendant or a stripper."

"A stripper?"

"Don't worry; your performance last night would've killed that theory even if you hadn't already told me you're a writer." He snickers, but he's not being mean. Playful, if anything. "You have really odd hours. I've noticed things about you too. You're not the only one who pays attention."

I don't know if that's a compliment or what.

"And you've been a good neighbor on one account, for sure."

"What's that?"

"You order a lot of Chinese food. It's gotten to the point where if you order, the restaurant calls me to see if I want anything too. And they waive my delivery fee."

"No fair!" It's really not either since those fees can add up.

He shrugs. "Next time you order lunch, maybe we could eat together. I work from home, same as you. It's lonely sometimes."

"Ha!" I blurt. "You're lonely? I've heard you going in and out at night. You've got quite the healthy social life going on. I can even smell your cologne sometimes. It's not hang-out-at-home-alone cologne. Let's not even get started on how my office is on the other side of this wall." I point to the wall in question. "And some of the girls you bring home aren't exactly quiet."

"Forget being a writer." He smirks. "You should be a detective."

"Funny." I smirk right back with a roll of my eyes. "And now that I'm thinking more clearly, why are you shirtless?" I wrap myself a little tighter in my—no, his—blanket and try to look as dignified as I can.

He looks down at himself, like he didn't know he was shirtless until just this second. "Oh, that. You puked on my shirt too. The one I put on after you passed out but before you decided to treat me to a clumsy striptease. I figured skin was easier to clean, so I'd better stay shirtless until I knew for sure you weren't going to spew again."

With that, he sits up and throws his legs over the side of the bed. Phoebe must hear the movement of the springs because she lets out a bark in response. "I've gotta go take Phoebe for her run. Don't forget to drink plenty of water today, okay?"

I don't have the chance to respond before he stands.

Oh boy. I wasn't prepared for this. He's wearing nothing but a pair of boxer shorts that leave little to the imagination.

And I'm a writer. I have a very good imagination. So good of an imagination in fact that I have to turn my back before the sight of Matt doing something as innocent as putting his clothes on makes my blood simmer dangerously.

The second he and Phoebe are out the door, I grab for the clothes folded neatly on a chair near the bed. They're freshly laundered and everything. *This guy … what's his deal?* I can't get a handle on him.

Now's not the time for that anyway. I grab the clothes and my computer, sitting at the bottom of the pile, and don't even bother getting dressed before hauling my embarrassed ass across the hall and collapsing into bed.

Maybe I'll get lucky, and by the time I wake up, my problems will have cleared themselves up. A girl can dream.

Chapter Four

THE SECOND TIME I wake up, the sun isn't a problem anymore. *Whoops.* I slept the day away. One of the benefits of being a full-time writer. There are lots of benefits to it really.

Except I can't think of any others off the top of my head since I have the same problem I had before I fell asleep. I have no product to sell to my editor.

There are a few texts on my phone, which came in while I slept, along with three missed calls from my best friend. I know Hayley's not going to stop calling until I acknowledge her, so I take care of her first while sipping a bottle of water. Matt was right. I need a lot more of this.

"You sound like you were asleep," Hayley observes within three seconds of answering. "You forgot to call me yesterday, you know."

"I did?"

"Sure! You were supposed to tell me all about the celebration at your editor's yesterday. So, how much bigger is your advance this time?"

Ouch. "It's ... not."

"Not bigger?"

"Not at all," I sigh. "It didn't go well. The whole day was one disaster after another."

I know better than to expect long-drawn-out professions of sympathy by now. Hayley's not that sort of girl.

"It sounds like you need a night out," she decides, and I can tell from her tone of voice that she's not kidding around. No excuses will be accepted.

Though I'm still tempted to give her one. *Do I really feel like going to the trouble of getting dressed up and socializing? Maybe she'll buy it if I tell her I'm sick.*

Except, physically, I feel better than I have any right to feel after the night I spent. Hours of unbroken sleep will do that for a person, I guess. And she's not wrong. I could use a little fun in my life after the events of the last day or so.

The well-timed growling of my stomach seals the deal. "So long as it includes dinner," I reply rather than turning her down.

She knows me well, rattling off where she wants to meet up like she knew in advance I'd make dinner my condition. "See you in an hour. Look hot."

Hmm. Hot's a pretty subjective adjective, but I'll do my best.

The trendy, new restaurant she named is nearby, so I have time to fuss with my hair and makeup after showering. Sleeping all day has its perks for sure since I feel much more clearheaded than I did yesterday before the drinking started.

If only there was a message from Maggie when I woke up, telling me she was wrong about my work, that everything would be fine. No such luck. I'm still stuck between a rock and a hard-on.

HAYLEY'S SITTING AT a high-top table near the bar when I arrive, and she's already surrounded by men.

I swear, if she wasn't my best friend, I'd hate her.

For one thing, she graduated at the top of our class in college and then did the same thing at Columbia Law. She's now working at a big Manhattan law firm while studying for the bar exam.

For another thing, she's gorgeous, hence the men crowding around in hopes that they'll win her attention. Long, shiny blonde hair. A megawatt smile, almost too perfect to be real. Big green eyes that can widen in innocence just as easily as they narrow dangerously.

Oh, and she has a body built for sin. Her words, not mine.

"There she is!" she announces loudly, waving a hand over her head.

I suddenly feel underdressed in my sequined tank and leather pants even though her clothes are more modest. She has the curves to fill out just about anything and make it look deadly.

"Kitty, this is Sean, Dylan, Drake, and Jackson," she rattles off.

It's amazing the way she can remember the names of four guys she met a few minutes ago while I need to meet a person at least a few times before their name is cemented in my mind.

The name Matt floats through my awareness, but that's different. He's unforgettable. Of course, the thought of him makes me remember this morning and the awkwardness from last night, and now, I wish I'd never heard of the man.

There's another reason I love her. It doesn't matter how crowded a bar is; Hayley can get a drink with no effort. She only needs to make eye contact with the bartender and twirl her finger around in the air, and then drinks appear like magic.

You'd think I wouldn't want to touch a drop after my lengthy visit with Mr. Patrón, but you'd be wrong. A martini is just what the doctor ordered.

At my first sip, Hayley shoos the men away. "It's girls' night," she announces with something that might pass for a pout. She doesn't apologize.

"I'll never understand your confidence," I have to admit. "I guess having every man you've ever met fall at your feet makes it easier to turn them away. You know there's always another guy waiting his turn."

"Oof." She grimaces. "It must've gone awfully bad yesterday if you're already this low. So, what happened? Did you not hit number one this time?"

Have I mentioned I also love her discretion? The gentle, delicate way she approaches a situation?

"I didn't hit at all," I sigh. It's not getting any easier to admit that. "The book was a flop."

"You can't win them all. Just write another one." She shrugs. When I gulp down the rest of my martini, she adds, "Does the publisher want you anymore?"

"In a word? No." I whirl my finger around like she does. "Could you use your magic to order up another? I feel like I could use it."

She leans in, brows lowering as she gets serious. "Listen, you're Kitty fucking Valentine. Get another publisher. Anybody would be lucky to have you! It's not like you're starting from scratch and you have no fan base, for God's sake."

"That's true …"

"Although I have to admit something." She frowns. "I enjoyed the book like I enjoy all your work, but I did end up wishing there were a little more sex in it."

I tap a finger to the tip of my nose. "Ding, ding! That's the problem. That's what they want. I need to write more sex. I need to write according to popular tropes."

"What's a trope?"

"You know, like a theme or a storyline used to identify a type of book. Or a type of main character, the sort of men women love reading about. There are popular tropes and unpopular ones. Here's a hint: I'm writing the unpopular ones."

Hayley wrinkles her nose. "Okay, so Maggie

wants you to write the popular ones. Like what?"

"Well, here's the thing." I have to lean in because this is way too humiliating to announce out loud in the middle of a restaurant that's growing more crowded by the minute as people get out of work. I'll either come off looking like a total weirdo or like a girl looking to score a date. I'm not sure which of the two possibilities is less appealing. "She asked me the last time I got laid. I was mortified."

"Ouch." Hayley cringes.

"She said I should start dating different types of men to use them as inspiration for each new book. She wants to serialize it, like a TV show or something. Can you imagine? And get this. She called them my sexcapades." I can barely get the word out of my mouth without gagging a little.

I wouldn't consider myself a prude, no matter how few sexual positions I've used in my life. *But sleeping around for the sake of writing books?*

Hayley takes a sip of her martini. She's a thinker, for all her beauty and charm. Men often underestimate her smarts, which sucks for them. I, on the other hand, appreciate her thoughtfulness.

"It gets worse," I continue. "The publisher wants to sell my new books for less than four dollars a pop. That's the literary equivalent of stripping—except once the publisher and Lois take their cut, I'll earn maybe a dime. I'm not even a stripper. Strippers don't work for dimes. I might as well panhandle on the street."

"Kitty ..." Hayley sighs.

"It's true! Do you know how many books I'd have to sell to earn a hundred thousand dollars?"

"A million," she fires back without even blinking.

"Right. And, if that's not bad enough, they want me to use my name. Kitty Valentine is synonymous with sweet romance. I feel like if I write something steamier, it needs to be under a pen name. Don't most strippers use stage names? Can't I even get that last bit of dignity." Maybe I'm feeling self-indulgent and morose, but I can't help it. There hasn't been enough time to wrap my mind around the situation.

"I'm sure some strippers do," Hayley agrees while reaching over, plucking her designer tote from the seat between us. She pulls something colorful from it and places it on the table.

"What's this?" I ask, eyeing it with suspicion.

It looks like a spinning prize wheel, only miniature, and there's a screen where I guess the names of prizes flash past until the wheel stops spinning.

Hayley folds her hands on the tabletop. "I didn't hear from you yesterday. I got worried. Then, I remembered meeting Maggie at one of your release parties. She gave me her card that night. I called her up, and she told me everything."

My jaw pretty much hits the floor. "Why did you make me repeat it then when you knew the whole time?"

"Because I wanted to hear it from you. How you're feeling about it. Literary stripping—it has a nice ring to it."

"Are you ladies talking about stripping?" A sexy waiter sidles up beside Hayley, and she giggles at his flirtation. "You two need anything besides a pole?"

I have no choice but to lay my head on the table in despair. I don't even have an appetite anymore.

Though Hayley doesn't know this. "We'll start with the spinach-artichoke dip," she announces. "Then, two burgers cooked medium. One with no bun, one with no onions. Fries. And another round of drinks."

I manage to lift my head off the table just enough to observe, "You ordered for me."

"Like I don't know exactly what you'd order by now." She smirks. "But you're in way too dramatic a mood to think clearly. It's not like you, Kitty. I know you love writing sugary-sweet romances, but this might be what you need to take your career to the next level. You could go from movies of the week to red carpets and box-office movie deals. You're a good writer. You have a fantastic imagination. But I have to agree with one thing your publisher says."

"What's that?" I ask with a sinking heart. Isn't it always easier to ignore compliments and focus on the negative?

"You need inspiration." She pushes the prize

wheel closer to me. "Which is where this gadget comes in. We're calling this dating roulette. After talking to Maggie, I did a little research and looked up who's hot right now. Each one of the types of men women want to read about is represented here. You spin the wheel, and the ever-wise wheel will tell you which type of man you're going to date and write about." She pats herself on the back. "Good job, Hayley. You're the best, Hayley."

She's adorable, and I love her, but I'm not quite at that point yet.

"I've been thinking about that, and it won't work. Readers expect happy endings in romance books. Even the super-sexy books. I'm not going to have a happy ending with all these guys."

I'm surprised her eyes don't fall out of her head as she rolls them so hard.

"Kitty! It's not supposed to be autobiographical. These men are inspiration. They're research. You'll write a happy ending for the characters in your book, based off you and the lucky fella you choose."

There's not a chance she'll ever lose a case. Not once she flashes that smile of hers, which she's turning on me right now. Full force. The girl could sell water to the ocean.

"Take a drink and then spin the wheel."

I would, but our appetizer arrives. Just when I thought I had no appetite left, the sight of so much creamy, cheesy goodness went and barged into my life. The server doesn't even have the plate set on the table yet before I'm grabbing for a warm tortilla chip and scooping an obscene amount. "I'm starved."

"Try to leave the bowl behind at least." Hayley smirks. "Come on. You're not leaving until you spin. Get to it."

And I will. First, I need another chip. I haven't eaten since … before the meeting with Maggie and Lois. No wonder I could eat even the less savory parts of a cow right now. I hope Hayley isn't committed to eating a majority of her fries when they get here.

"I'm not easy to be friends with, am I?" I can't help but ask, looking across the table at my best friend.

She's wearing a slight smile, like she's just on the right side of amused but on her way to genuine irritation at the way I'm stalling. "What makes you ask that?"

"I don't leave my apartment for days on end. I get so wrapped up in my work that I forget where I left my phone half the time. But you never give me grief for it."

"Maybe because I'm just as hard of a worker as you are," she suggests with a soft laugh. "I can relate."

True, and now that she's landed the role of paralegal to one of the firm's partners, she'll be working longer hours than ever. The fact that she managed to find time to sit in a restaurant with me is a small miracle.

"Thank you for taking the time to do this for me." I smile. Here I am, complaining and stalling, when she was kind enough to call Maggie and go to all this trouble. "I appreciate it so much."

Another winning smile. "Okay, I'll fess up. I had one of the assistants make it up for me. What can I say?" She laughs when I roll my eyes. "I'm good at delegating. Though I did go through and remove anything I knew you would've turned down flat."

"Like what?" I have to ask since I'm turning the wheel and watching as one trope after another goes past. *There are so many! How could she have removed any?*

"Being a breeder, for one." She snickers with a wrinkled nose. "No need to bring a baby into all this. No married men."

"Huh. It's funny that you actually found married men as a trope since romance is generally a no-cheating zone."

"Well, I took it out anyway." She shrugs. "Oh, and I figured a shifter or vampire might be tough to find, even in Manhattan."

I can't help but laugh along with her. *Maybe this won't be such a big deal after all. I can do this. Right? What's the worst that could happen? I might even have a little fun.*

"Here goes nothing," I whisper, closing my eyes and flicking the spinner.

"Ooh! You got Boss." She claps. "You get to date

your boss! How exciting will that be?"

"Hang on. Wait up." I laugh, waving my hands around. "I can't date my boss—or rather, Maggie's boss, which I guess means my boss. He's married with three kids, and he has a belly and only half a head of hair. I just can't—"

"No, I'm talking the big boss." She holds up her phone, where she was typing something in while I whined. "Blake Marlin, CEO and billionaire. Your publisher is only a portion of his media conglomerate."

Blake Marlin. Sure, I've heard the name. Who hasn't? At the tender age of thirty-two, he's managed to amass a stunning empire. Magazines, blogs, newspapers, radio and TV stations. Hayley's right; book publishing is only one small part of the larger whole.

He's also handsome as anything. Big, soulful brown eyes. A killer smile. His sandy-blond hair is tousled in the picture she's pulled up, like he just ran his hand through it. He's an avid sportsman, and his fit body and tan skin reflect this.

"He's a little too hot for me." I shrug. "And fabulously wealthy. Why would he want to go out with me in the first place? Besides," I add when it looks like she's about to slap me silly, "that's two tropes in one book. Boss and billionaire. They should be separate. Right?"

"I don't know. What's your imagination tell you, Kitty?"

"That I need to spin again. Can't I start small the

first time?" I ask, hands clasped in prayer. "Maybe just this one time, I can choose my trope rather than spinning for it. Let's see … there's bad boy, best friend's brother …" I shoot her a sly grin.

"You know as well as I do, that would never work," she warns. "He's too deep in his frat-boy days right now. You'd practically be robbing the cradle."

"He's twenty-one," I tease. *Let's see how she likes it.*

She doesn't. "Moving on."

"Okay, okay. Hmm. Firefighter, single daddy, cowboy, rock star, doctor, motorcycle club, actor, prince/royalty, lifeguard, race car driver, foreign lover, tattoo artist, police, boy next door … there are so many!"

I have to laugh since I'm nowhere near halfway through the list. My social life's about to get pretty interesting.

Then, another option catches my eye. "Hot Santa?"

She waves a hand at me. "I added that. I thought it would make a fun holiday edition. Plus, you'll get to sit on Santa's lap and tell him what a naughty girl you've been."

"Do you have any idea what the chances are of actually finding a hot Santa?" I ask with a giggle. "Maybe a dancer in a Santa costume, but the type you see at the mall? Normally not that hot."

"You're the writer." She shrugs as our burgers arrive. "You'll figure it out."

Chapter Five

HERE'S THE THING about Blake Marlin, CEO of Marlin Enterprises. Billionaire extraordinaire. General hottie with a body.

He's not technically my boss. I mean, he is, but not really. He's been tangentially responsible for my career, but even that's the thinnest thread connecting us. I'm sure, to him, I'm small-time. Nothing important. A girl who writes romance books. He'd probably assume I was some starry-eyed cat lady if he ever gave me a moment's thought, which I doubt he ever has.

This is my way of trying to talk myself into dating him—or rather, approaching him and seeing if I can lure him in. Hayley's words. She wouldn't let me choose a new guy—big surprise—convinced Blake is not only the natural choice, but the easiest of all. Otherwise, I'd have to go out into the world and search for a single father or police officer to date, and that would take a lot more time.

Time I don't necessarily have. While I'm not completely frivolous with the money I've earned—I save for retirement and a rainy day and all that—I can't afford to go too long between releases for more reasons than just finances. An author is only as good as their next book. Readers nowadays tend to take a *what have you done for me lately* attitude toward even their favorite authors since self-publishing lends itself to rapid releases. People have started to believe that's the way all writers should work when it just isn't possible for many of us.

I can't let my name wither on the vine, in other words.

"And he's speaking at a media conference in two days," Hayley informed me over our burgers the other night. "You can get in at the last minute—if anybody can, you can. Maybe Lois could help. I'm sure you'll think of something to catch his attention."

"But what?" I groaned, a French fry hanging half-way out of my mouth.

"Oh, definitely eat like a slob. I know I'd be turned on if I liked women." Hayley snickered. "Earth to Kitty. You're the romance writer. You always write little meet-cutes in your books. How do you come up with those?"

"There's a big difference," I countered. "I can control what both parties say and do and think. I can't control what Blake thinks of me or whether he wants to go out with me."

"Don't worry," she assured me. "I'll give you a few pointers. You wanna know how to get a guy's attention and keep him hooked? Look no further."

So, here I am, in a car on my way to the hotel where the conference is underway. The keynote speaker is due to make his presentation today. None other than Mr. Marlin himself.

"Why is this so important?" Lois said when I—gasp!—called and asked her to do something an agent normally did.

"Because I want to meet a few industry professionals," I fibbed while pacing my office. "I need to keep my options open right now, Lois, what with things being in flux at the publisher."

She managed to score me a pass into the conference well after the tickets had sold out, so I guess I owe her a floral arrangement. I make a note of this in my phone before referring to the list of tips Hayley gave me.

Don't be too open. Men like mystery.

Let him chase you. Men like to feel like they're in charge, especially wealthy, powerful men.

Toss your hair a lot.

I roll my eyes at this one, though I deliberately left my hair down today. *Do men really go for that?* I always figured that was some sort of a silly generalization, but maybe there's something to be said for it after all. If it works, I'll have to put that in my new book.

It's been a long time since I've flirted. Shamefully long even. I've spent way too much time wrapped up in work. Sometimes, I even forget the day of the week when I'm good and busy.

How does a person catch the attention of a billionaire?

Actually, my first problem is getting into the conference room where he's speaking. It's standing room only at the back, rows of chairs between me and the stage set up at the far end.

What am I supposed to do? Set myself on fire? That'll get his attention.

"Excuse me," a man murmurs as he brushes past.

At least he excuses himself or even acknowledges my presence. I've been nudged aside and ignored more times in the last few minutes than I can keep track of. It's mostly men here. They're not exactly thoughtful or observant, these guys. One thing I've learned over the years of researching men and their habits for my work: true alphas aren't rude, especially to women. They might be forceful or brusque, but they wouldn't shove a girl aside to claim a seat.

The lights in the room dim right on time, just as the stage lights brighten. Moments later, a handsome young man strides out onstage, and the room erupts in respectful applause. I join in because, well, the guy's practically a legend at the young age of thirty-two.

And because, holy moly, he's even more gorgeous in person. Whoever came up with the idea of placing screens around the room so those of us in the back could see him was a genius and probably deserves a bouquet larger than the one I plan to send Lois.

There's only so much a photo can convey. Magnetism isn't one of those qualities. And the man has it—in spades. I can barely keep track of what he's talking about, as I'm so busy noticing the dimple in his left cheek, his obnoxiously long eyelashes— *seriously, what's up with men having thick, lush lashes? How unfair is that?*

Instead of being forceful and loud, the way some of the men around me were speaking just before the talk began, he's friendly. Even playful. Serious about business, no doubt, but if he ever decided to give up being a mogul, he could make a mint as a public speaker.

He's a leader, in other words, and I can practically hear the audience soaking up every last word as they scribble on notepads, type into their phones and laptops. Poor them. They don't get to watch and admire the way his eyes twinkle when he makes a joke.

Then again, maybe they're not as interested in his sparkling brown eyes as I am.

How in the world am I going to catch those eyes and hold his attention? He's spectacular while I'm … me. Hayley would be much better at this than I am. I should've sent her. That would've been a better idea! She could do the dating for me, and I could write about it.

Though she's already spent enough precious time helping me out. I should send her flowers too. Maybe I'd do better by buying a florist shop.

The talk lasts an hour, after which time Blake answers questions sent his way prior to the conference. Some of them are really funny.

One guy asked how he finds time to sleep with all the work he must do, and he responds, "My best work is done in the bedroom ... asleep—for anybody out there getting the wrong idea."

I don't know about that. I wouldn't mind hearing that deep, rich voice murmuring my name while he ...

Oh jeez, I should be taking notes. He's giving me all kinds of interesting ideas I think my readers might enjoy.

He's finished all too soon. I could listen to him speak forever. He could read a menu, and I'd hang on his every word. Except I still have no idea how to catch him.

I have to dash out of the room to beat the rush, hoping I can catch him outside in the hall. He's supposed to be having a meet-and-greet with VIPs—aka people who spent extra money to upgrade their experience.

Lois wasn't able to score me that sort of ticket though, so my best chance is either before or after that session. I'll toss my hair a lot, make sure he knows how mysterious I am. Like I don't even care that he's super rich and hot as a ten-alarm fire—

The next thing I know, I'm hit from behind. My purse flies in one direction, and I fly in the other, landing on my knees on an uncarpeted floor. I hear people crying out in surprise and concern all around me while my knees scream obscenities and blood rushes in my ears.

"What the hell?" I gasp, looking up through the curtain of hair I was hoping to toss in Blake's direction. I can't tell who hit me as they rush past, but it doesn't matter. The result was the same, no matter who did it.

"Are you all right?" a man asks, crouching in front of me.

I can only see his shoes, shiny and expensive-looking. He reaches for me, and there's no missing a Rolex on his wrist. Terrific. I made a huge fool of myself in front of a rich guy who happens to be the only one nice enough to stop and ask if I'm okay.

"Nothing hurts but my pride," I mutter, looking around for my purse. Thank God it was zipped or everybody in the hall would have been treated to a wide array of chewing gum, mints, lip glosses, and feminine hygiene products. That would've been the cherry on top of a half-melted sundae.

"Let me help you," the man offers, taking my arms and practically lifting me onto my feet. He's strong but gentle—though I have no time to reflect on either of those attributes since I soon learn it's not only my pride that's busted.

"Oof," I groan the second I put weight on either

leg. Neither knee is bleeding, but there are already bruises coming up.

"I wish I'd caught up to the guy who slammed into you," my savior growls. "But I was a little too concerned with helping you. I'm sure there are security cameras all around here. If you want, I can have the footage examined."

"Why would they …" I start, finally getting up the nerve to look Mr. Helpful in the eye. It's not easy since I feel about as clumsy and awkward as I've ever felt, but I manage it.

Brown eyes. Ridiculous lashes. Tan skin, sandy hair, the sort of jaw that brings to mind a comic book superhero.

"You're Blake Marlin," I whisper, forgetting the pain in my knees and my pride for a second.

His smile widens. "And you're my special guest for the rest of the day. Come on. Let's get you into a chair." As he helps me into the smaller conference room where his VIP event is scheduled to take place, he calls out, "Can somebody grab a couple of ice packs?"

That's the thing about the very wealthy and very powerful. They don't even have to direct their requests to anyone in particular. They just know they'll get what they asked for.

Chapter Six

"REALLY, THIS ISN'T necessary," I insist as Blake helps me into a wheelchair. A freaking wheelchair. Somehow, he managed to get one for me, so I wouldn't have to walk. "I'm sure I'll be fine."

"Yeah, well, those swollen knees tell another story," he sighs as I settle in. "I've twisted both knees before, playing sports. I know how much it hurts, and I know how important it is to stay off your feet."

"I've been sitting all afternoon," I remind him with a smile.

I watched from the sidelines, ice on my knees and my feet up on a chair, as he held the special meet-and-greet with several dozen attendees. One of them kept shooting guilty looks my way, and I'd bet anything he was the one who'd knocked me down.

But that's okay. He did me a favor even if he doesn't know it.

Blake crouches in front of my chair, where I'm trying my best to look dignified. "You know something? I don't even know your name. You know mine, but I was rude and never thought to ask for yours."

"Oh." I laugh. "It's okay. I didn't think that was rude at all. You had your event to get to." I hold out a hand, which smarts like heck after landing on it along with my knees but I think I can withstand a shake. "Kitty Valentine."

"Not *the* Kitty Valentine," he murmurs, brows lifting almost clear off his forehead. "Kitty Valentine, the author?"

"Um, yes? I mean, yes. That's me. Sorry." I laugh, and now, I want to put that aching hand over my face to hide how hard I'm blushing. "It's just that I would never expect you to recognize my name."

"Are you kidding? You're a phenomenon—four best-sellers over four years."

I can hardly believe this. "I'm sorry. Did I hit my head when I fell? Because I'm having a hard time believing you know anything about my career."

His smile widens. "I appreciate success, especially in the form of a phenom who's good enough to send the competition running for the hills. You managed to surprise the publishing world with how quickly you rose through the ranks, and your talent speaks for itself."

"Don't tell me you've read any of my books." That would truly be too much—and the final nail in my coffin. No way I'm conscious and clearheaded if the man professes a love for sweet romance. I must've knocked myself out when I fell.

Darn it, he's hotter than ever when he blushes.

"To be honest, no, I haven't."

"I thought so." I grin.

"But my sister has. She's a big fan of yours, and I trust her taste over just about anybody else's." He tilts his head to the side. "You write for one of my publishers, don't you?"

Dang it. Of course, he was bound to make the connection. Soon, he'll be brushing me off, telling me it's nice to have me on board or whatever. I can't tell him about my woes either or he might think I'm trying to get my next book picked up by heading straight to the top of the food chain.

It would also reek of desperation, and nobody wants to date the desperate girl.

"I do." I smile. "Happily. Everybody's been so good to me."

"That's what I like to hear." He stands, thrusting his hands into his pockets.

Even now, completely relaxed, he's breathtaking. Smiling down at me, backlit—thanks to a fixture just behind his head. It creates an aura around him, like a halo. I'm surprised I don't hear angels singing.

"Mr. Marlin?" A young woman trots over, pointing to the screen of her phone. "Your jet is wheels up in forty-five minutes."

"Right," he sighs. Then, he winks down at me. "But that's the nice thing about having your own jet. You get to decide when to leave." Strange how something that might've sounded totally … well, douchey, coming out of anybody else's mouth, is cute and charming, coming from him.

"But your dinner plans," the girl murmurs.

"Right." He nods, his jaw tightening. "Okay. But first, I'm seeing this young lady home—if she lives nearby, that is. I don't know if a drive out of state is in the cards today."

"Oh." I blush, even as I wonder how to wrangle a date out of him. Not that the sight of him and the sound of his voice aren't enough to inspire a virtual porno film of scenarios in my head, but I could use a little insight into his life. "I live here in the city, but you don't have to do that."

"I insist." And he doesn't sound like a man who's used to being disagreed with. "It's the least I can do for a best-selling author who happens to write with one of my publishers. You've had a rough day. Let me see you home."

When I hesitate—because honestly, his generosity is staggering—he adds, "You'd better make up your mind quick or else I'll be late for my flight and for an important dinner. You wouldn't want that."

It's the way his mouth twitches like he's trying to hold back a laugh that does me in. No matter how sexy a man is, the sexiest thing of all is a sense of humor. Hands down.

"Okay, okay, I don't want to make you late."

"Great. Let's head out to my car then." He turns

to his assistant. "Please make sure my bags are on the jet and let the pilot know I'm running slightly behind schedule. Oh, and please, call home and let her know I might be a few minutes late but not to go calling the police or the hospital. I had a slight bump in my schedule."

Her? Home? My stomach drops. I thought he was single, but it's not sounding that way. He has dinner plans with his wife or girlfriend. Whoever she is, she sounds overprotective. *Darn it! All this effort and humiliation for nothing.*

"Come on then, Kitty Valentine." Blake grins, taking the handles of the chair and actually, honest-to-God pushing me out of the room and down the hall.

Blake Marlin, the billionaire, is pushing me in a wheelchair, and he might as well be Moses parting the Red Sea. The people around us step aside without needing to be told, gaping with wide eyes and murmuring to each other. *Who's the girl in the chair? Why in the world would a man this powerful be pushing her wheelchair?*

"They probably think I'm a charity case," I mutter under my breath.

But not quietly enough.

"What's that?" Blake asks, chuckling.

"Nothing. So, uh, where are you heading tonight? Someplace fabulous, I'd guess. A fancy restaurant?"

"Hardly." He snickers as he continues to push.

We're near the front door finally, so I won't have to endure being stared at much longer.

"Come on," I tease. "You? Then again, I'm sure what you consider everyday and ordinary would be spectacular to somebody like me."

"To the famous Kitty Valentine?" He chuckles as we cross the sidewalk with a hotel concierge at our heels—probably to get the wheelchair once I'm out of it and to generally grovel at Blake's feet.

"I'm famous in a very small circle," I remind him when we reach the black limousine parked at the curb. Of course this is his car. There I was, thinking he'd be the one driving.

The driver climbs out and opens the door while Blake helps me to my feet. It's not a bad attempt at flirting that has me leaning against him, though having the excuse to do so is nice. His chest and arms are just as firm as they look in his suit. If I didn't feel like my legs were screaming, this would not be the worst afternoon I'd ever had.

"I'll tell you a secret," he murmurs as he helps me into the limo.

His cologne is intoxicating, the sort of scent that makes me want to bury my face in his neck. *I need to remember this feeling for when I'm writing.*

"What's that?" I ask, scooting over to make room for him.

He slides in beside me with a sigh. "I'm having dinner at my mom's house tonight. That's where I'm going. Now, you know the truth about me. I have to catch my jet, so I can get to my mother's house. Shh. That'll be our little secret."

I wonder if he's looking for somebody to fall in love with him because I'm halfway there. "You're kidding. Dinner at Mom's? So, she's the one who might call the hospital if you don't show up on time?" That would explain the overprotectiveness anyway.

"Correct. I love her, I do, but she hovers. Even now. Especially now really since I'm always traveling. Don't I know how dangerous air travel can be? That sort of thing."

"I'm sure it's out of love."

"Oh, undoubtedly. It's just that nobody tells you when you hit the so-called big time that your mom will still see you as a little boy." He laughs.

What a laugh. It's like warm honey pouring over me and sweetening everything around us.

He turns on the seat, facing me. "What about you? What made you want to become a writer?"

I clear my throat. *Should I tell him the whole story?* Hayley told me to be mysterious, but he's already interested in knowing more about me. If I act coy now, it might turn him off.

"To be honest, I couldn't find a guy in college who lived up to my hopes and dreams, so I decided to write him."

"Really?" He folds his arms, looking me up and down with a sly smile. "Maybe I should start reading your work after all."

"Why do you say that?"

"I'd like to know more about your hopes and dreams when it comes to men ... to see how I measure up."

Son of a ...

"Oh," I breathe, and it's a wonder I can get that much out, considering how my heart's pounding like a runaway train.

"Of course, that's presumptuous of me. You probably have a boyfriend."

"I don't," I blurt out much, much too loud.

He chuckles. "Good for me then. What do you say?"

"To what?" Good Lord, he's going to change his mind by the time the ride ends if I don't get it together. It's just that, at some point along the way, I forgot I'm supposed to be doing this for my career. Maybe it was when I almost shoved my face in his neck.

"To having dinner with me some night soon. Maybe in a few days? I should be back from a conference in Miami on Tuesday. How about Tuesday night?"

"That sounds wonderful," I have to admit, and it does. It sounds too good to be true actually. Dinner with Blake Marlin. Talk about the sort of situation a girl only dreams about.

"Great. I'll give you a call," he promises as we pull up in front of my building.

Darn it, that was a quick ride. I could easily spend

another hour sitting here, talking with him. Longer than that if given the opportunity.

But I do need to get upstairs and ice my knees, and he needs to get to his mom's. How adorable is he?

"I insist," he says as he helps me up the stairs.

I don't even have it in me to argue. Not only is he my knight in shining armor, but without his help, I also would've had to crawl up on my butt like a baby learning how to walk.

When he leaves me standing by my door, whistling as he jogs down the stairs, I wonder if I'll have it in me to date anybody else after Blake Marlin. Because I could see myself falling for him.

And to think, I didn't have to toss my hair once.

Chapter Seven

"WHEW!"

I didn't even hear Matt enter the hallway behind me, probably because my heart's pounding out of my chest and I'm trying really hard to keep myself from sweating the makeup off my face.

It's not hot in the hallway.

It's that I'm on my way out to meet up with Blake. I'm surprised I've slept at all in the last three days, obsessing over every last detail. How to do my hair and makeup, whether to get my nails done, what to wear. Especially what to wear.

I settled on a classic Audrey Hepburn effect, a little black dress and heels—my knees are in much better shape after three days of rest, so I can wear the Pradas I save for special occasions. My grandmother's pearls are at my throat and ears, and my long, loose waves are swept over one eye and down one shoulder.

What I don't need right now is a commentary on how I look, but something tells me that's what I'm going to get.

"Don't you look special?" He grins when I turn

away from locking my door. "What's the occasion?"

"I'm going out to dinner." I shrug. "No big deal."

"No big deal. You're serious?" He looks me up and down in a very obvious way, and I find myself liking him less than I did last week. Probably because I don't enjoy being teased the way Matt's teasing me now.

"What about it? Just because I'm not drunk on Patrón and stripping my puke-stained clothes, you don't know what to think?" See? I can laugh at myself. "I'm not always such a mess."

"I wasn't trying to say you were." He laughs. "Boy, you're touchy tonight. Yet another reason I know this is a special event. You're nervous. Tense."

"Wasn't it you who said I should be a detective rather than a writer?" I smile, though my teeth are clenched. "Because you're showing some skills yourself."

"Cute." He snickers. "Anyway, I just wanted to say you look nice. That's it. Because you do."

"Thank you," I sigh.

I shouldn't be so snappy. He does live across the hall and everything, and he was awfully sweet to me when he could've been anything but.

"I'd better get going. I don't want to be late."

"For your date," he calls out behind me as I start down the stairs.

"Not a date!" I lie over my shoulder.

"Yeah, okay." His laughter follows me all the way down.

Why do I feel the need to lie about what this is all about? I have no idea. Because it's certainly a date. Just because I'm doing it in hopes of writing a book the publisher will actually want to buy has nothing to do with it.

If anything, I reason as I walk out to the curb, *I can laugh about this in the future.* How I ended up meeting Blake after a professional disappointment. It's written in the stars, our finding each other. If it hadn't been for the market being the way it was, we would never have had a reason to cross paths.

Well, the market and whoever knocked me over at the hotel.

"Oh, there you are."

I turn in surprise at the sound of a deep voice and find Blake walking toward me with a bouquet of red roses in one hand. My favorite. He couldn't have known that, of course, but the fact that he was thoughtful enough to bring flowers just about melts me into a puddle.

And boy, howdy, is he looking good. He's wearing a dark blue suit with a starched white shirt underneath, unbuttoned at the top. I can smell that cologne of his, even at a distance, thanks to the breeze blowing my way from behind him. *Gosh, he's overwhelming.*

"Hi! I'm sorry. I thought we were meeting at the restaurant."

"I should've been clearer. I want to take you there for dinner, but of course, I planned to pick you up. I'm not the best at communication," he admits with a boyish grin. "Ironic, I guess, considering what I do."

"It's okay. And these are beautiful," I add, indicating the roses.

"Oh, these? They're not for you."

"Oh," I whisper.

He bursts out laughing and hands them to me. "Of course they're for you."

"You probably think I'm slow on the uptake, huh?"

Maybe if I bury my face in these flowers, he won't notice how embarrassed I am. I need to remind myself that he's a normal person. Just a guy. I don't have to be so self-conscious around him.

Should my heroine be self-conscious too? Yes, if she's a normal girl, and he's her billionaire boss …

Now's not the time, Kitty. Right. I can think about the writing later.

Now, I'm standing in front of what is essentially a unicorn. He's utter perfection. I can't allow myself to get lost in the future and lose what I have in front of me.

"Thank you," I whisper, breathing deep.

The flowers are lush, the biggest I've ever seen, and almost unbelievably red.

In other words, I don't think he got them from around the block or at a gas station. This wasn't a last-minute purchase.

"Are you hungry?" he asks, leading me to the car. It's not a limousine this time, just a regular old town car, but there's still a driver involved.

"I wasn't able to eat a bite all day," I confess as I slide into the car.

"Oh, that busy?" he asks.

"Sure was." Lies and more lies. I was too busy freaking out about what tonight would be like. My stomach could barely handle water. But I'll let him think I was busy working my fingers to the bone.

He joins me, climbing in on the other side, and nods like he understands too well. "The price of being successful. It's been a long time since I've met a woman who knows the feeling. There's this misconception out there that when a person has enough ... wealth, they can sit around and twiddle their thumbs all day. How do they think that wealth was earned, you know?"

"But you earned it," I point out with a gentle smile. "You didn't inherit it. Maybe that's the problem. They assume you didn't work for it."

"Now, how do you know I didn't inherit my money?" he asks with a smirk. "I don't exactly go around, bragging about my life. I can't stand braggarts, honestly."

"That's nice since I can't either."

So I did my research. So I know he's a self-made man. Yes, he inherited a little bit of money when his father died at a young age, but Blake was smart enough to have a manager invest it for him. At the age of fourteen, he knew just what to do.

By the time he graduated with a master's degree in business ten years later, his inheritance had quadrupled, thanks to aggressive, high-yield investments. It was enough to buy his first two publications. The rest, as they say, is history.

And a lot of hard work. *There's a reason he's still single. Not many women have the fortitude to put up with a man they barely ever see.* I can't help but hold that thought in the back of my mind as we cruise down Manhattan streets.

"More reason for me not to be one, if you don't like bragging." He looks down at my legs, and for a second, I wonder if he realizes he's checking me out so openly. Until he asks, "How are those knees? I didn't notice a limp."

"Oh, just fine, thanks. I probably would've been in much worse shape if it wasn't for you making sure I didn't have to do much walking. I doubt anybody at the hotel would've cared half as much if it wasn't for you being there."

"Let's say, I believe in helping a damsel in distress." When his phone rings, tucked in his breast pocket, the grin slips off his face. "Excuse me. I have to take this."

"Of course." I turn my attention to the buildings going by outside the window.

It's a beautiful night, and I'm in a car with a billionaire. We're on our way to dinner. I can hardly believe my luck or my life.

Don't forget to add this in the book, I think, wondering if taking notes on my phone would be rude.

Nah, not a good idea. I don't want him thinking I'm taking notes on him personally, like I want to gossip to everybody I know. I'd imagine that being as wealthy as he is—his word, *wealth*, which is definitely on a different level from rich—means paranoia. At least a little.

"Okay. Sure. Set it up for tomorrow morning. Well, he'll have to deal with it. Some of us wake up before noon. Let me know." He hangs up a moment later, and I almost feel bad for being in the car with him. He seems upset.

"Boys' night out?" I ask with a tiny smile.

His smile's wider. "The opposite. Business stuff, nothing interesting. There's another thing about me that you should know: I don't have much patience for people who balk at the thought of an early meeting."

He puts the phone away, though I notice he doesn't silence it. I guess that's another drawback to being a powerful person. He can't ever be off, so to speak. He can't relax.

He helps me out of the car when we reach the restaurant, which comes as no surprise. It's like he came from way back when, the days of chivalry.

"I never would've imagined being able to get a reservation here," I have to whisper as we enter what's probably the trendiest, hottest restaurant in the city.

"Having a well-known name helps." He shrugs, like it's nothing. Like the fact that all he has to do is wiggle a finger and his needs are all taken care of is something just anybody could relate to.

I like how normal he wants to be.

Though he'll never be normal. The eyes following us into the restaurant and through the dining room are just one indication. Just when I'm starting to wonder what it'll be like to eat dinner while being stared at, I find us entering an empty side room holding exactly one table.

"I figured we'd want a little privacy," Blake explains. "I hope you don't mind. Not everybody enjoys having their every move watched."

"I appreciate that," I whisper with a laugh. A little shaky, a little nervous. "What do you think about it?"

"About what?" He pulls out my chair with a grin.

"About having your every move watched."

He shrugs a little as he sits. The candlelight plays off his perfect features. There I was, thinking he couldn't get handsomer than he already was.

"In everyday life, it fades into the background. It has to; otherwise, a person might lose it. I can't spend all of my life worrying about who's looking at me, if somebody's watching, whatever."

"I can understand that. It would be beyond unnerving."

"I'd never get anything done. I've heard of people having breakdowns over that sort of thing. Then, on top of everyday life, there's what happens whenever I have a deal in the works, or I've been seen with a new girl. Everything gets turned up to eleven, if you know what I mean."

"That must be terrible. I question myself enough of the time as it is. I'd have a breakdown if people were watching me all the time."

"You'd better be careful then," he teases. "You'll be in my shoes one day. Just keep writing those books of yours." Suddenly, he leans forward. "Though I don't know who you'll be selling those books to since, from what I understand, your sales have been slowing. Painfully so."

So, this is what happens when a person truly feels their stomach drop. I've used that expression more times than I care to imagine, but I never understood it until now.

It's not so much what he's saying but how he's saying it. He looks and sounds like a snake preparing to strike. And he was such a sweetheart just a minute ago. He's a good actor.

"So, Kitty Valentine"—Blake smiles, teeth flashing in the candlelight—"it's time you lay your cards on the table. Why are you really out with me tonight?"

Chapter Eight

I PROBABLY SHOULDN'T wipe my sweaty palms on my dress, but what other choice do I have? My hands are shaking. So's the rest of me.

"What? I don't understand." And that's not a lie. Everything flipped upside down so quickly; I don't know which end is up.

"You don't understand? Are you sure about that? Because all it took me was a few minutes of work to learn about you. To really learn." He folds his hands in front of him, his features settling into neutral lines. "So, tell me why you went out of your way to get my attention at the conference. The real reason. Because if I were a betting man, I'd say you want me to find a way to get your next book sold. You don't want the publisher to drop you after your abysmal sales."

"Hang on a second," I whisper. Oh goody, my voice is shaking twice as hard as my body. "You're wrong about that. I mean it. I fell because some guy slammed into me from behind. That's it."

"You mean to tell me, it was nothing more than chance that brought us together? Mere days after your editor got an advance copy of the *New York Times* Best Sellers list, and you weren't anywhere near it?"

"This isn't me trying to sell a book, I swear." This is a nightmare. "Why couldn't you tell me before going to all this trouble of bringing me out and everything?"

"I wanted to see if you'd be able to go through with it. Which you did. I must admit, you have a good poker face. I would never know you were trying to use me to score a lucrative new deal."

"It's not true. Did somebody tell you that? Because they're wrong. I thought … I mean, you were so sweet to me at the conference, and you've been so great until now that I figured …"

"You figured." He blows out a low whistle. "You still refuse to tell the truth."

"I'm telling the truth." There's no choice but to get out of my chair since I won't sit here and be stared at like I'm lower than street scum. So much for learning to enjoy the finer things in life. So much for telling my grandchildren one day while sitting on my yacht or whatever that I met their grandfather through the strangest of circumstances. "I'm sorry if you can't get it through your head, but I'm not doing this to get a book deal from you. That wasn't on my mind at all. And you know what else?"

I'm vibrating with rage now, gripping the table since I can't grip his throat. "I feel sorry for you, period. You have to be so paranoid all the time. You have to jump to conclusions about people and be mean and cold because you think they're using you. It means you've been used before, and that's a shame. You seem like a nice person otherwise."

"Thank you." He smirks.

"I'm not sitting here and letting you abuse me when you're completely off base," I spit in his general direction before turning on the heel of a shoe this guy didn't deserve to see. I can't believe I broke out the Pradas for him.

"Hold on. Hold on." He's in front of me in a second, brow furrowed in confusion. "Are you serious? You didn't do this to score a new deal?"

I fold my arms and glare up at him. "I didn't do it to score a new deal. I'm not trying to use you. I admit, I wanted to meet you the other day. And I wanted you to ask me out." Why not tell the truth now? I might as well.

His frown deepens. "Okay. So, why didn't you bother to correct me when I praised your success?"

"Well, I mean, I used to be successful. I wasn't about to give you a sob story about how bad things have gotten recently. I didn't want you to think I was doing exactly what you just accused me of doing."

"This has nothing to do with work then?" He places his hands on his hips, and now, the corners of his mouth are tugging upward. He's trying not to smile.

I would hate to ruin that smile, but I'd rather not go through this again. It's not an easy decision to make really. Because I want him to like me. I want this date to go well. And not only because of the book I'm supposed to write based on our interactions.

"Well, maybe just a little bit, and please, don't get mad at me again," I squeak in a tiny little voice, squinting until my eyes are practically closed. "I need to write something new. Something different. My editor's sick of sweet romance, which is what I write. She suggested I ... start dating around. Expand my horizons and all that."

"So, she suggested you go out with me? To improve your writing?" He cocks an eyebrow. "That sounds ... strangely wrong, but I can't put my finger on it."

"She didn't suggest you in particular," I sigh, throwing my hands into the air. "Just different men."

He doesn't need to hear the word *sexcapades*. That would take this night from a moderate disaster all the way to, like, the perfect storm of catastrophe.

"So, you're doing this for your career, just not the way I thought." He strokes his chin. "And you're going to write about me?"

"Not you. Not even me. Two different characters, but ... yes ... based on ..." I point to him and then myself, back and forth.

"Is it true you were asked to write dirtier

books?" Now, he's straight-up smiling. "Hey, when you're the big boss, you can find out anything you want to know."

"Oh. Oh!" My face basically bursts into flames. "We're not—I mean—you know. I'm not trying to write about that sort of thing. We don't have to …"

"Come on." He snorts, taking my elbow. "Let's sit down. I want to hear more about this. It might be the only thing I've had a good laugh about today."

He's in a better mood now, thank goodness. More like his usual self.

"I've pretty much told you all there is to know," I sigh, sitting again. "My editor pointed out that my worldview is fairly limited. I can't keep writing the same stories again and again—obviously, as proven by my latest book sales."

I stop short of burying my face in my hands, only because I spent a lot of time on my makeup and hair and would rather not ruin both.

"I'm sorry things have gone downhill for you. Really, I am," he insists when I shoot him a dirty look. "Like I said, my sister's a huge fan, and she's got good taste. Clearly, you have a big fan base or else you wouldn't have already sold so many books."

"The publishing world is fickle."

"You're telling me?" He leans back in his chair with a sigh. "At least we're being up-front with each other now. That's a relief. I would like to get to know the real Kitty, not the version of Kitty who feels like she needs to be prim and proper just because I own a few companies."

"A few companies?" I have to giggle just a little. "Hating braggarts is one thing, but there's such a thing as undervaluing yourself too much."

"But you won't deny, you were acting a little stiff and self-conscious."

"Who doesn't act that way on a first date, for Pete's sake? And excuse me, but you're the first wealthy man I've ever gone out with—no, even better, you're the first wealthy man I've ever met. I mean, you're a billionaire. With a B. There aren't that many of you in the world."

"I'm just Blake." He spreads his hands. "What you see is what you get."

"Keep telling yourself that." I smirk. "It's not that simple. You're bound to make a girl uncomfortable, Blake Marlin. But not in a bad way. Never in a bad way."

"In what way then?"

I cover my stomach with my hands and then flutter them around. "Like there's butterflies in there."

He smiles from ear to ear, and I notice his eyes are twinkling again. "That's different. I wouldn't want to think you were uncomfortable in other ways."

"Just a minute ago, you were ready to rake me over the coals," I remind him.

"Just a minute ago, I thought you were a mercenary, failing author who thought she could butter up the boss and convince him to pull strings for her."

"Fair enough. Now? What do you think now?"

He at least pretends to think it over, tapping his chin and barely hiding a grin. "I think we need to order something to eat since I've had a hell of a long day, and I have to admit, I've been concerned about this dinner all throughout."

"Same here," I groan. Some of that fluttery feeling in my stomach is probably hunger.

"And I would love to hear more about this plan of yours to learn more about different men. Different types of men, I'd guess," he adds. "I guess I'm just one of so many, bound to have their hearts broken in service of your career."

"Wow. You have a way with words." I have to laugh when a server comes our way with a bottle of champagne and a bucket of ice.

"I'm in media," he points out with a wink. "I know all kinds of words. And just because I don't read sweet romance doesn't mean I don't read."

"So, you're more than just a pretty face, huh?"

"I should hope so since my face isn't all that pretty."

I have to bite my tongue or else risk asking if he's ever looked in a mirror. Maybe he needs to get his eyes checked. Maybe he needs a driver because his vision is poor.

Blake hands me a flute of fizzy champagne and

then holds his up to touch mine. "To teaching you all about the way billionaires live," he announces.

"To what now?" I almost forget to take a sip; I'm so surprised.

"Teaching you how billionaires live." He holds my gaze over the rim of his flute, and there's humor in his eyes.

This is better than him accusing me of being scum, but I can't say I love feeling so off-balance, thanks to this sudden change in the conversation.

"Is that what you plan on doing?" I ask, practically holding my breath as I wait for his answer.

"Why not?" He places the flute on the table. "Go on. It's bad luck not to drink after a toast."

Now, it's my turn to eye him, but I'm feeling suspicious. *Wow, this is excellent champagne.* I've been drinking swill at Maggie's office, but I didn't know any better. He's spoiled me forever.

He waits until I'm finished before explaining, "It makes sense to me—at least from a business standpoint. You need to see how the other half lives if there's any chance of writing a book about … is this about a boss or a wealthy man?"

"Either, or," I admit. "Both?"

"Fine. You want to see how billionaires live? I'll show you. You'll have an entire series worth of material by the time we're finished. Your book sells well? That benefits me too. See? It's a win-win all the way around."

If his little pitch didn't sway me, the sexiness in

his smile would do it. He's feeling naughty now, which adds an entire layer of deliciousness to what's already pretty delicious on its own.

"You would do that?" I'm not quite sure I can believe him, but maybe I'm too jaded. Maybe I need to adopt a little of the romantic optimism I've been writing about all these years.

"Why not? I enjoy spending time with you. You're intelligent, driven. Beautiful."

"Stop," I whisper as my cheeks burn.

"And you're real. These last few minutes, with the two of us talking openly and honestly, have been some of the most refreshing I've spent recently. Since, come to think of it, the last time I was with you. I'm starting to think you're the common denominator, and I need to take advantage of the fact that you fell into my life."

"No pun intended?"

"Oh, pun absolutely intended."

I have to laugh. "I would never say this under any other circumstances, believe me, but I can hardly wait to see what you have to offer."

There goes that dimple in his cheek and the twinkle in his eye. "I hope you can handle it."

I hope I can too.

Chapter Nine

I KNOW THIS sounds ridiculous, but writing a book can bring to mind the pain of childbirth.

Not that I've ever birthed a child, which is why I feel ridiculous, making the comparison. But I can't help it. As I sit at my desk, staring at the blinking cursor, which somehow gives the impression it's judging me, I wish I had an excuse to let out a primal scream of agony.

It's not exactly writer's block, but it might as well be.

In the two days since my first date with Blake, I've been an incredibly productive person. My apartment is cleaner than it's been in forever. I rearranged the books on the shelves that line my living room, something I do from time to time when I decide I'd rather have them grouped by color or by title or by author. I watched a bunch of YouTube videos on deep cleaning, like using a lemon half-covered in kosher salt to scrub away the hard-water stains on my kitchen sink, and then went to work. I even emptied the fridge and wiped down the shelves.

In other words, I've gotten no actual work done, but at least the place smells like lemon. It's a small consolation, but I'll take whatever I can get right now.

If only I knew how to start things off. *How does my billionaire boss know the heroine? In what capacity does she work for him?* My ceiling holds no more answers than it did this morning or yesterday, yet I'm staring at it again. I can't make their relationship mirror the one between Blake and me. I need to fictionalize it.

An assistant? That's a popular one. Yes, she's the boss's assistant. Her name is Phoebe for right now since Matt's dog tends to bark and run around just when I'm deepest in thought. It's like she knows I'm trying to concentrate and wants to mess with me.

She's succeeding.

How do things take a turn between Phoebe and her boss? I try going through a bunch of possible scenarios before wondering if I should keep it simple and make it reality adjacent, if not exactly the same as to how we met up in reality. *They're going to a conference together.* Simple enough.

But then what?

When my phone buzzes with a new text, I practically jump on it. Anything to avoid the pain of trying to figure out the details.

So? How's the writing going? Hayley asks with a bunch of smiley faces and prayer hands.

I guess that means she's excited for me but also praying I don't fling my laptop out the window, quickly followed by myself.

It's not, I have to admit with sad faces and chocolate bars, indicating just how much candy I've consumed over the last couple of days.

While I normally try to eat healthy food and I'm still sticking to my daily yoga practice, stress tends to make me crave chocolate. *I don't know how to do this. What even is writing? What are words? Maybe I need a new career.*

You know who you remind me of? she asks.

Who? I ask, curious.

Yourself, she replies. *Every time you hit a snag in whatever you're working on, you start questioning every decision you've ever made in your entire life, and I have to remind you what a fabulous writer you are and how you'll work your way through this problem the way you work through every problem.*

She's right, and I hate it. I always get all self-doubtful when the work goes slowly.

But this isn't slow. This is stagnant. This is wondering when things are supposed to heat up between my hero and heroine—and how. After all, things between Blake and me haven't heated up yet, and I'm not sure when they will.

Or if they will.

He hasn't been in touch with me since Tuesday night.

A chaste kiss on the cheek was how he left things on dropping me off. "I'll think up something big for us to do next time," he promised with a cryptic smile before heading back out to the car.

Only there was no indication of when next time would be.

He's a busy man. I have to keep that in mind. Trying to steal time with him will be like ... well, trying to steal time. Whenever he has a break in his schedule, he might be able to devote some of that time to me. Or he might not.

My imagination is going to have to fill in the blanks.

I crack my knuckles and decide to write. It doesn't have to be great. It doesn't even have to be good. But I have to get words down regardless.

Bubbles tickled her nose when she raised the flute to her lips. "This champagne is delicious," Phoebe offered after taking a sip.

"Do you drink a lot of champagne as a rule?" Bryan asked.

Yes, Bryan's a good name to start off with, though I almost never stick to the first name I choose. *Big Boss Bryan. Maybe that's what Phoebe calls him when she talks about him with her best friend. Hmm ...*

Phoebe had the sense he was teasing and didn't know how to react. "Whenever I can," she quipped with a little smile, tossing her hair over one shoulder.

See? I got a hair toss in there.

Yes, yes, the scene is starting to come together. I see them sharing dinner in his suite after the conference has wrapped up for the day. Oh! Maybe it's a weekend-long event, and they explore the city together—or rather, he shows it to her because, obviously, he's been there. He's been everywhere.

If only I knew how things would go between Blake and me, I might have more confidence in this.

Bryan's firm, full mouth spread in a slow smile. "Maybe I'll teach you the finer points of champagne, so you'll know better what to order the next time you have the opportunity," he suggested. "It's the least I can do since you do so much for me."

She knew he was joking. That he didn't expect her to order champagne. After all, he paid her salary. If anybody knew how far below the champagne-and-caviar line she fell, it was her boss. Sure, he was generous but not that generous.

"Yes, I'm sure they have an excellent selection at the bodega down the street from my apartment," she replied smoothly, smiling all the time.

That got him. His smug attitude popped like a balloon once he knew she was on to his little game. The sense that she'd won a small victory gave her confidence. He wasn't the only one who could play.

He recovered quickly, pulling another tool from his legendary arsenal. "A woman as beautiful as you? As smart and witty? You should have men falling at your feet, begging to show you the world."

Yes, there was that charm she'd heard so much about, having never seen proof of it before now, except while watching him sweet-talk a client or prospect.

"If I said yes to one of those men, who would pick up your dry cleaning and keep your appointments straight?" she asked with a slight shrug. "I'd hate to see you show up late for a big meeting, wearing a dirty suit."

"You think I'm completely lost without you? Is that it?" Now, his smile was wide. He was genuinely, sincerely amused by her. Not by the word games he wanted to play, not by the thought of making her squirm after lavishing compliments on her. "What if I showed you how capable I am? What if I'm the one to show you a thing or two this weekend?"

I sit back with a sigh, nodding. *And how would Phoebe react to that? How did I react when Blake suggested he show me how people in his world lived?* I pretty much almost fell out of my chair. *How would Phoebe feel though?* The stakes are higher for her. She works closely with this dude.

Only how do things finally heat up? And what is it that's keeping them apart? Does he think she's a corporate spy? Or does he get wind of a counteroffer made to her at the conference by a competitor? Somebody who wants to steal Bryan's top asset—his beautiful, brainy assistant—so they can undermine him while learning all his secrets?

What is this, a spy thriller? It's supposed to be a romance. I know I need to take more time to read up on what's popular right now, so I can have a sense of how to structure this, but I've been too busy deep-cleaning my bathroom grout with baking soda and vinegar.

Maybe I should've chosen another profession. Writing is like tearing my heart out and placing it on the page for all the world to see.

My notes from my date with Blake, scribbled down after the fact and barely legible, don't help much. Nor do the notes I scrawled after the first time we met, which I wrote with my feet up on my desk and ice packs on both knees.

Because no matter how deep I dive into the characters and their feelings and the way my hero makes the heroine's panties melt with just a single glance, one hurdle remains—the sex. I have to write sexy times for them while all I've gotten from Blake is a kiss on the cheek.

I grab my phone and fire off a quick text to Hayley. *What do you think about me watching porn for research purposes? Maybe bondage? Or an orgy?*

The last thing I expect is an almost-immediate reply. *I think you should be careful about texting me things like that during work hours since I was just showing my boss something on my phone when your message came through.*

I bury my face in my hands and wonder if it's possible to literally drop dead of embarrassment. *Sorry, sorry. Please tell him I'm sorry too.*

She doesn't get back to me this time. I can't imagine why …

Still, porn is not a bad idea. I have to get new

ideas going. I have to familiarize myself with various kinks and positions. *What if Big Boss Bryan has a kink he only feels comfortable revealing to Phoebe since she's that special woman with the vagina powerful enough to heal him?* Sure, and he's such a control freak, so it could be something to do with dominating.

"Note to self," I mutter as I type into my web browser's search bar, "clear your search history." Not that it matters. I've done research on so many strange, offbeat things over the years that I'd be surprised if I wasn't on an FBI watch list by now.

That's another thing most authors probably have in common. If we ever banded together during an apocalypse, we'd survive based on all our shared bits of random knowledge.

Where to start? "Domination," I murmur as I type the word and am instantly assaulted by dozens and dozens of thumbnails leading to one video after another. Right away, I can tell this isn't for me since some of these women look like they're in serious pain. "No way is that a turn-on," I whisper, horrified at the sight of a woman's breasts bound in leather straps until her flesh is purple.

But it must be hot for some people, right? Men, I guess, or women into pain and humiliation. I don't know that this is the audience I'm writing for. I'd better come up with a different search term.

"Handcuffs," I suggest next.

And voilà, all the handcuffs a girl could want.

Fuzzy, leather, iron shackles. A girl with her ankles cuffed too, and the chains connecting each cuff is then connected by a third chain.

Hmm. This strikes me more as erotica, and I'm not writing that.

What the heck am I writing then?

I click on one video that looks to be at least good quality. There's not that homemade vibe about it. In one thumbnail, for instance, there are baby toys off in a corner and a laundry basket full of onesies. Actual onesies, not adult-sized. It seems viewers aren't too discerning when it comes to how their smut is produced.

"Oh, yeah!" the girl screams within moments of the video starting up, and I almost have a heart attack because I forgot the sound was even on, much less turned up so high. "Fuck me, Daddy!"

"Shh!" I hiss, horrified, fumbling for the volume control. Only I manage to knock the laptop off my desk, sending it crashing to the floor. It stays in one piece, and the video keeps playing. I almost wish I'd broken it.

"Punish my ass!" she shrieks just before I hit the mute button, leaving the handcuffed girl screaming silently while the man in question does indeed punish her ass.

I'm frozen, eyes bulging, lips pressed together, and staring at the wall between my office and Matt's bedroom. If there is any good in the world, if there is a chance of a benevolent higher power existing somewhere in the universe, he's not listening. He's somewhere else. In his living room or out for a walk with the dog.

To my growing horror, I'm pretty sure there's soft laughter coming from the other side of that wall. I could be imagining it, but I don't think so.

Chapter Ten

IT'S EARLY EVENING, but the noise from the street below my building is just as boisterous as ever. I lean back on my hands, tilting my head to catch the last rays of the sun. I suppose I'm a recharging battery. Maybe this will help my imagination start spinning again.

It was never this difficult before, mostly because I wasn't stretching myself. I understand that now. It's fine and wonderful to write exactly what I like, for the situations and words to flow smoothly because the subject matter is near and dear to my heart.

And even then, it's not like writing has ever been super easy. It comes with challenges, even on the best days. On the hardest days? Like, if I'm not feeling my best or my hormones are off the charts or it's been raining for several days in a row? Forget about it. I might as well be slogging through semi-set concrete.

This is unlike anything I've ever been through before though because the pressure is higher than ever. My first book was written practically as a lark, something to do in my free time. I only queried it because Hayley had read it and said it was worth-while; otherwise, it would've been forgotten on a hard drive. After that, I sort of coasted on the success of my debut.

Now? I might as well be starting from scratch.

"What are you doing up here?"

I close my eyes at the sound of Matt's voice. It's not an unwelcome sound per se, but I'm a little too busy brooding to want to get into a deep conversation—or even worse, a playful one. I'm not feeling particularly playful at the moment.

Especially now that he knows I've been watch-ing porn with the volume turned up. I can hardly wait for him to make fun of me over that one.

"I didn't know it was off-limits," I call back over my shoulder.

"It's not." He comes closer. "I've never seen you up here before, is all."

That gets my attention. I sit up, wrapping my arms around my knees and watching while he heads straight for the far corner of the roof, near the ledge. "You come up here a lot?"

"When the weather's nice, yeah." He shrugs. To my surprise, he pulls a folding chair from seeming-ly out of nowhere, tucked under the ledge and in the shadows.

"And you have your own chair? Boy, I never thought of that."

"For a writer, you need to open your mind up a

little." He drops a wink, unfolding the chair nearby. "You want it? Please, by all means."

"Nah. I'm okay on my blanket." Though I will definitely bring a chair up next time. *What a good idea.*

He takes a seat, manspreading, as men so often do. He's wearing a T-shirt and jeans with holes in the knees and no shoes.

"What if you stepped on something dangerous up here?" I ask, horrified at his bare feet.

He wiggles his toes like he's pleased with himself. "What could there be?"

"I don't know! And neither do you! I mean, for Pete's sake, it's New York. Anything's possible."

"I like going barefoot," he explains with a shrug, "whenever possible. It's a thing of mine."

"You know, I just realized something." I look him up and down, perplexed. "I never asked what you do for a living. How come you work from home? Are you a flight attendant? Or a stripper?"

I expect him to laugh at the reminder of his original ideas about me, but he looks penitent instead.

"Yes. You've figured out my dirty little secret."

"You're a stripper?" I whisper, suddenly more interested.

His face falls further. "A flight attendant."

I can't help but laugh. "Ooh. Scandalous."

He laughs along with me. "Okay. It's much less of a secret than that. I manage large banking portfolios."

"Oh? That sounds—"

"Don't even pretend you think it sounds interesting." He snickers. "Nobody finds it interesting, except for those of us who do it. And it is interesting really. I wake up before dawn to check out the foreign markets and run reports, which I then analyze to see if I can tweak an investment strategy here or there. The US markets open at nine thirty. I usually have time to take Phoebe for her run before then, and I settle in for work after that."

"But you've already been working since before dawn."

"Technically, yes." He shrugs. "You're not the only one who works odd hours. Except I'm usually getting up at roughly the time you go to sleep."

"How would you know when I go to sleep?"

"You're the one who pointed out the thin wall between your office and my bedroom. There are mornings when I hear you muttering to yourself in there. I guess you're acting out the dialogue you're writing or something like that."

Oh, the horror. I have to grimace. "No. Really?"

"Hey, it's nice to wake up to that sort of thing. Love talk or whatever you wanna call it. Though it does get a little sticky-sweet sometimes. No offense."

"None taken. Remember, that's the big problem I'm having right now. Stepping away from that and into something … rawer. Grittier. But still captivating, still something that'll hook my readers."

"Is that why you're up here? To think things out?"

I nod, miserable again. "I usually go for a walk in the park, but I already walked earlier today, and it didn't help anything. I thought a change of scene might get the juices flowing."

"So, you can get the juices flowing on the page?" When I shoot him a look that can only be described as withering, he holds up his hands in a defensive gesture. "Sorry. Probably not the time for jokes."

"Maybe not," I agree, though I have to snicker in spite of myself.

He's only trying to be friendly. It does seem strange that after a year of never seeing him, we've run into each other three times in one week, but I've come to accept that this is the way life works sometimes. Hayley's super busy, and I can't bring myself to bother her, so the universe sent me someone else to bounce ideas off of.

If I could only get past the fact that he's so stinking handsome. It's not easy to separate the man from his hotness. Familiarity and the passage of time should help though. I'm already less tempted to blush every time our eyes meet. It might have something to do with the fact that he's seen me at my worst and still bothers talking to me.

"How'd your date go the other night?"

He would bring that up, wouldn't he?

"Not as well as yours did later that same night," I singsong with a simpering smile. "Thin walls."

"I swear, if I end up getting distracted by wondering if you're listening …"

"I'm not actively trying to listen to the screaming banshees you bring home," I assure him, rolling my eyes. "But it gets loud. I wish I couldn't hear it."

"Earplugs?"

"A pillow over the face?" I counter.

"Only when she's into it."

"What?" I gasp, eyes bulging.

"Would you chill?" He laughs. "I've never asphyxiated a partner. Don't go getting the wrong idea. Some things even I feel uncomfortable with."

"What do you not feel uncomfortable with?" I have to ask.

"Are you sure you wanna know? Have you had enough to drink?"

"Okay, okay. I'm not a complete novice, you know. I'm no blushing virgin."

"No, but you have the blushing part down pretty well." He grins, pointing to my face. "Like right now. And don't pretend you didn't avoid answering my question about your date. How did it go?"

"Why does it matter?"

"Because I almost never hear you leaving the apartment, especially not at night. Which tells me you don't do a lot of dating. Didn't you say your editor asked when you last got laid?"

"I told you that?"

"You did." He nodded, solemn. "Anyway, I figured it was a big deal since you looked like a million bucks."

"I did not."

"You kinda did. Learn how to take a compliment." He folds his hands over his flat belly and raises his eyebrows. "Well? How'd it go? Who was the lucky guy?"

Fine. He wants to know so badly? I'll tell him. We'll see if he believes me. "What if I said I had dinner with Blake Marlin?"

His brows almost disappear under his hairline. "I'd say I've underestimated you. The Blake Marlin? Billionaire Blake Marlin?"

Bingo. I had a feeling he would know the name if he works in the financial world.

I raise a finger. "Media mogul Blake Marlin. You forgot that one."

"Right, right." He scrubs a hand through his hair, leaving it disheveled. "Wow. What the heck does Blake Marlin do to impress a girl?"

"It was only dinner. Really," I insist when he cocks his head to the side. "And it was nice. I ended up having to come clean about why I was out with him, but …"

"Pardon? Why you were out with him? Why would you be out with him aside from the obvious boy-girl dating thing?"

Oh. Right. He doesn't know about this. "Well … I needed to fulfill a certain trope I'm going to write about."

"Blake Marlin is a trope?" He bursts out, throwing his head back with his eyes closed.

I almost forget to be annoyed with him in favor of marveling at how impossibly handsome he is.

"You know what tropes are?" I ask once he's finished laughing himself sick.

"I know things. I'm not all numbers and currency exchange rates," he retorts. I'm surprised he doesn't stick his tongue out. "So, you went out with him because he's rich?"

"Wealthy," I correct without thinking. "And yes. That was the general idea." I leave out the whole boss part. Something tells me he'd fall off the roof and chuckle the whole way down if I mentioned it.

"And he figured it out? That sucks." He doesn't look or sound like he thinks it sucks. He's too busy chortling over my bad luck.

Which is why it gives me pleasure to correct him—that, and the fact that he's a little too smug for his own good. "Actually, he thought I was using him because of his money and connections. I set him straight. He appreciated me trying to revive my career and promised to give me plenty of material to use."

I expect Matt to at least make a dirty joke.

His deep scowl comes as a surprise.

"What?" I finally have to ask. "It all works out. I don't have to feel so nervous when we're out together because I'm not putting on a pretense of trying to get him to like me while hiding the real reason I need to date him."

"This doesn't strike you as being sort of ... wrong?"

"How is it wrong?"

"You're dating a man just so you can write about the things you do together. And he's okay with this?"

"It's not like I'm using him," I argue.

"But you are. You're using him as research, and you'll make money off it."

"So will he!" *Darn it.* I throw my hands over my mouth, gasping as my eyes bulge.

Matt's eyes, on the other hand, narrow. "What's that mean? Are you giving him a cut of the profits? Is this even more uncomfortable than I imagined?"

"He ... kinda, sorta ... owns my publisher." I brace myself, closing my eyes and waiting for the grief he's bound to deliver. "Go ahead. Give it to me. Tell me what a rotten person you think I am."

Instead of chiding me, he starts to laugh. Again. "This is the wildest thing I've ever heard. And I've heard some wild things."

I open one eye just a little. "Yeah, I've heard them too. Through the wall between our apartments."

"Kitty, I wish we'd started talking a lot sooner because you're a breath of fresh air." He runs his hands over his eyes like he's wiping away tears of laughter. "Good luck with dating your billionaire boss. I can hardly wait to see how things turn out in your next book."

"I'm glad this is so funny for you. The fact that my life brings you laughter warms my heart."

"You might wanna be careful how much you drink around him," he warns with an edge of laughter still in his voice. "I know from experience. And something tells me his rug is much, much more expensive than mine."

"I'm happy to pay you for that, by the way."

"We'll call it even since I've saved so much in delivery fees from the Chinese place," he offers.

"Oh, right. Yeah, we're even." I scowl. "And I have no intention of making an idiot out of myself in front of him. I need him too much."

"And when you have enough research, you can drop him in favor of the next guy." He gives me a thumbs-up. "Really, you've perfected what we men have been trying to legitimize for a long time: an excuse to date with no strings attached and then dump 'em when we're through."

"That sounds downright mean."

"No hard feelings." He shrugs. "The girl I brought up here the one time didn't seem to mind."

"What? You … up here? Like, out in the open?" I know it shouldn't gross me out, but I can't help it. "Ew, Matt! Here I am, worried about you walking around barefoot, when you've done a heck of a lot more than that with even less on!"

"Aw, you were worried about me being bare-foot? I thought you were only getting off on bossing me around."

"Hush." I don't feel right, sitting here anymore, knowing he and some random girl got it on probably right here. Sure, countless rains and snows have happened since then—I guess anyway since asking for details would be weird—but still. "I should get back to work."

"Are you feeling better about it than you did when I got up here?" he asks, getting up and folding his chair while I fold my blanket.

Am I feeling better? Strangely enough, yes. Much better. "I needed to get out of my head for a little bit, so yes. Thank you. I was starting to brood too much."

"Then, I'm glad I decided to come up." He grins before replacing his chair. "And I'm dying to find out how this goes. You'll have to give me all the details."

"Hush, I said."

"But it's like a soap opera. Or a reality show. I'm already hooked."

All he gets for this is a tongue stuck out in his direction before I turn away.

"Oh, before I forget," he calls out to the back of my head, "hit me up the next time you want to watch porn for research, and I'll point you in the right direction. I can't imagine you writing a character who begs Daddy to punish her ass."

That is when I push him off the roof—at least, that's what I imagine doing while he laughs softly behind me.

I'm glad he thinks this is so funny. For me, it's real life. What if I burst out laughing at a stock market crash or something that would affect his job and make life crazy for him?

My phone is buzzing as I enter the apartment. I need to remember to bring it with me when I go out—one of the things Hayley's always getting on my case for.

There's a text.

From Blake. *Free on Saturday night?*

I can't help but grin like an idiot. A Saturday night date. Everybody knows that's a huge deal.

Sure! I reply, and then I instantly wonder if the exclamation point was a bit much. I don't want to come off as being too eager. And crap, I answered in less than a minute. *Way to look desperate.*

Good, Blake replies. *I'll pick you up at your place at six. Be ready for a big night.*

A big night? My hands feel all tingly as I type out my reply, assuring him I'll be ready. In the back of my mind, I can't help but think how this will show Matt he doesn't know what he's talking about.

This is going to go perfectly.

Chapter Eleven

"ARE YOU FLIPPING serious?"

Probably not the smoothest thing that could've come from my mouth. Not even close really. But how else am I supposed to react when we pull up beside a sleek jet?

Blake laughs. "I love how open you are."

"You do?" I feel a little skeptical. I'm the girl who's constantly putting her foot in her mouth.

"Sure. It's refreshing. You're refreshing." He pats my exposed knee, and I notice the way he lets his hand linger just a second longer than it needs to.

Not that I mind. Not even a little bit. He looks and smells so delicious; it's taking a great deal of my self-control to keep from jumping into his lap. I mean, while I need things to go in that direction—a peck on the cheek isn't much to work with, and that's all I've gotten so far—I can't imagine him taking it well.

Refreshing or not.

"You didn't tell me we were flying somewhere," I point out while climbing from the car.

"I wanted it to be a surprise. Besides"—he grins,

taking my hand and leading me to the stairs—"it's not like we're going halfway around the world. Don't worry. I'll have you back safe and sound."

"Who's worried?" I laugh, though it sounds shaky, even to my ears.

"You are. I can tell."

He stops before we reach the bottom stair and turns to me, taking my other hand so he's holding both. He has a firm grip but a gentle one. I can't help but remember how heroic he was when I fell and how safe I felt, thanks to him.

"This was just an idea, you know. You said you needed information on how wealthy people lived. Research, right? But if you're feeling nervous, it's okay. You can take a look around inside the jet, jot down a few notes for reference, and then we can go someplace else." His thumbs slide over my knuckles. "Whatever you want."

No, we cannot do whatever I want since what I want when he murmurs that way and looks down at me with those twinkling eyes of his is to drag him up the stairs and join the Mile-High Club, though I suppose we'd have to leave the ground to make it official.

Is it possible? Could he be as perfect as he seems? "I want to see what you have planned for this evening," I decide. After all, nobody ever got anywhere by being too cautious. And in spite of myself, I can't help but look back and recognize how cautious I've been. Cautious to the point of coasting on my past success, unwilling to stretch and grow. This is as good a start as any.

That is how I end up seated in a butter-soft leather chair beside Blake, sipping champagne, which just so happened to be chilled and waiting for us.

"It's incredible," I murmur, looking around.

"The champagne or the jet?" he jokes, winking.

"Both, smarty-pants. Is this good champagne since I'm such a plebeian when it comes to these things?" I tease right back.

He holds up the glass like he's examining the contents. "This is a 2008 vintage," he explains. "That was a very good year—one of the two best years of the aughts."

"I should be taking notes, shouldn't I?"

"I'd be glad to remind you whenever you'd like."

His eyes meet mine as he takes a sip of the fizzy liquid. Now, I feel all fizzy inside too. He has that effect on me.

"I'll have to take you up on that." I finish off the glass just as we're about to take off. Good thing, too, since I can't hold a champagne flute while gripping the armrests like my life depends on it.

"Oh no. You're afraid of flying? Why didn't you say so?" Blake asks, concerned and clearly upset.

"It's not the flying that bothers me," I confess, eyes closed. "It's the taking off and landing. Those are the two most dangerous times."

"For what it's worth, I spend a ridiculous amount of time in the air, and I'm still here." One of his hands closes over one of mine. "We'll be okay."

And I believe him. He has a way about him, an energy that instantly calms me. Maybe it's his confidence, his self-assuredness.

"Have you always been this way?" I ask through clenched teeth as the world pulls away from us—or rather, as we pull away from the world.

"What way?"

"So sure of yourself? Does that come with success, or is it the other way around?"

"You mean, has my attitude led to success?"

"Yeah, that's what I mean."

"That's a funny question."

I have to open one eye to look at him. "I hope I didn't insult you."

"No, not one bit." Though the creases in his normally smooth forehead say otherwise. "It's just that I've never thought about it before. I guess my personality is what it's always been. Yes, to a degree, I've always been sure of myself. I knew I was going to be successful."

"Did you imagine this level of success though? I'm sorry if I'm asking too many questions," I add in a hurry. "Sometimes, my curiosity runs away from me. You don't have to answer anything you don't want to."

"Why would I not want to? Now, if your idea of

getting to know me better involves sharing my Social Security number, that's when we'll have a problem." He snickers.

"Hold on. Let me make a note of that …" I mime writing a note on my palm. "No … Social … Security … number. You know this is going to make my life a lot harder, don't you?"

"Cute. But I mean it. You don't have to feel sorry for being curious. I'm curious about you too."

"Yeah, but you can go into my records with the publisher and learn just about everything you want to know. Including my Social Security number."

"Oh, I already have," he assures me with a wave of his hand.

"Good luck with trying to steal anything." I laugh. "You won't get far." Besides, I'm sure that the savings I've worked so hard to put aside would be like a drop in the bucket for somebody in his position.

"That's not the same as knowing a person though," he points out, and he's serious now. "Learning what a person likes and what they don't. Where they've always dreamed of visiting. What the name of their imaginary friend was when they were a kid, if they had one."

"Emily," I confide without blinking.

"Mine was Fred. I used to talk to him before going to sleep at night," he replies. "I think he lived inside the wall next to my bed, but I'm not sure. I was never clear on it. Anyway, that's the sort of stuff I want to know about you."

"I have to admit, I'm finding it hard to believe you'd want to know anything about me. No, I'm not fishing for compliments," I add when he scoffs a little. "I'm a normal person. I'm not that special."

"Not that special? A *New York Times* best-seller four times over by the time you turned twenty-five? You don't think that's special?" The corners of his mouth twist upward. "Trust me. I've seen more failures and fizzles than you could ever imagine. Do you have any idea how unique you are?"

"Okay, when you put it that way, I sound completely out of touch, like I take my success for granted," I admit. It doesn't make me feel very good either.

"I'm sure you don't. You're too down-to-earth. But not everybody lives on the Upper West Side. I mean, I grew up just outside Philly. Mom would've stayed there if the doctor hadn't told her she'd do better to live in a drier, warmer climate. I'm still a Philly boy at heart, right down to the teams I follow. And I've eaten in five-star restaurants around the world, but there's nothing so good as a cheesesteak from Jim's."

"I've never had one," I admit.

"You're kidding."

"I'm not."

"We'll have to change that."

"I can hardly wait." And that's a fact. I'd go just about anywhere with him. Which brings me back to the present moment. "Where are we going?" I have to ask. "You never did say."

"Oh, right." He laughs. "I thought we could have dinner in Chicago."

"Chicago! You can do that? Just decide on a city where you want to have dinner?"

"Sure." He shrugs like it's completely normal. "I have an apartment there for work anyway, and one of my close friends is the executive chef at probably my favorite steakhouse in the entire world. I hope you're in the mood for meat."

Lord, how my cheeks burn. For somebody who hates writing about graphic sex, I sure do have a dirty mind. If he notices, he's nice enough not to make a big deal about it.

"Yes, I could go for … meat," I manage to say before my throat closes up.

Wait a second. Did he just say he has an apartment in Chicago? Is that the endgame? Inviting me to spend the night?

It occurs to me that I wouldn't mind. Not one bit. And not only because I need to research.

When he offers more champagne, I can't help but accept. It's time for Kitty Valentine to stop writing about exciting romance and start living it for herself.

Even if I accidentally dribble some champagne down my chin when Blake's not looking. I'm nothing if not consistent.

Chapter Twelve

"I'M GOING TO have to get a thesaurus," I whisper.

"Why?" Blake asks with a smile.

"Because I need new words to describe everything you're showing me. Amazing, incredible, awesome … I'm getting tired of hearing myself say the same thing over and over."

But I can't help it.

The restaurant is located in the basement of an old hotel, where it used to function as a speakeasy back in the days of Al Capone.

"This was a favorite hangout of his," Blake explains when we pull up in front of the grand, old building with its wrought iron railings and elaborate plasterwork decorating the front.

Rather than go in through the double doors, we take a narrow flight of stairs down to the basement and are greeted by a beaming young man introduced as the restaurant's executive chef. He gives us what he promises is the best table, situated in the back corner of the room. It's intimate for sure, a high-backed booth that leaves us semi-removed from the rest of the diners.

"Does this seem commonplace to you?" I ask once the wine is poured and we're alone again. A nice, full-bodied red to complement the steaks we haven't ordered yet but probably will. The aroma of seared beef is just about enough to knock me sideways.

"Not even a little bit," Blake assures me, raising his glass. "Especially when I get to show it all to you. I guess even the coolest, most exciting things would get boring without somebody like you to share them with."

There I go, blushing again. "By all means, show me whatever you want."

"Oh, I will." He grins with a wicked gleam in his eye.

For Pete's sake, will I ever stop walking into the double entendres? At least I manage not to choke on my wine. Barely.

I turn to the menu, looking for an escape or at least a change in subject. "Blake?" I whisper, glancing up at him.

"Yeah?"

"There aren't prices next to anything." Craning my neck to peek at his menu tells me I didn't get a misprint—unless we both did.

"I know."

"So, how do you know how much you're going to pay for things?"

He's such a sweetheart, trying so hard not to laugh out loud at how ignorant I am. "Here's a secret about restaurants like this one: if you have to ask, you probably can't afford it."

"Oh." I feel roughly two inches tall now.

"Not to brag or anything like that," he continues. "You know how I hate it. But that's the way it is. And if you think this is something, wait until I take you to a chef's tasting. There's a restaurant back in Philly that I absolutely adore. Thirteen courses, beautifully plated, just exquisite."

"Thirteen? I feel full, just thinking about it. How long does it take?"

"Three or four hours, typically. You sit at the chef's table inside the kitchen and watch each course as it's prepared. It's an experience from beginning to end. I think you'd love it."

"I bet I would."

What I really love is knowing he's planning future dates. Sure, we started this from a sort of professional angle. He's scratching my back, and he knows it.

But he's interested in me and interested in going out again. I can't pretend not to be flattered.

"Tell me a little more about you," he urges, leaning in ever so slightly.

We're in a rounded booth instead of one that leaves us facing each other, and there are only a few inches between us.

Is it the champagne from the jet that has my head spinning a little? Or maybe it's the sense of so many new, exciting things happening at once.

There's a definite energy in this underground space with its exposed brick walls and crystal chandeliers. I wouldn't be a bit surprised if the ghost of Al Capone himself walked by, a cigar hanging from his mouth and a moll on one arm.

More likely, the spinning head has to do with the man sitting next to me. He looks good enough to eat, and I'm not only thinking that because I'm starved. Tonight, he's wearing a well-fitted black button-down, snug against the muscles of his biceps and chest. I have to remind myself not to lick my lips as my gaze travels over him.

"What's there to say?" I ask, shrugging a little.

"You already told me why you started writing romance," he muses in a soft voice. "Where do you come from? What's your best friend's name? What do you like to do on a rainy day?"

"I grew up in New York," I explain. "I can't imagine living anywhere else in the world. It's messy, yeah, and noisy and crowded. But I'd probably lose my mind if I lived someplace quiet. No traffic, no voices." It's enough to make me shudder.

"I completely agree." He nods.

"My grandmother's family is old money," I admit. Why does it make me uncomfortable to talk about this? "She sort of disowned my mom when she and Dad eloped. He was working-class, and my grandma hated that. We lived in a two-bedroom apartment in Brooklyn until I was ten. Dad got a promotion, and we moved into our own house. It was great. I think Grandma Dolores got over it after a while once she saw how hard he was willing to work to provide a good life for us. Plus, it helped that Mom had named me after my great-grandmother, who was the family matriarch."

"Her name was Kitty?"

"Kathryn," I correct. "Kathryn Antoinette."

His mouth twitches. "That's quite a name."

"I've never gone by it, except in Grandma's presence. Mom always called me Kitty. Anyway, Grandma was generous enough to set me up with a fund for college. I know how lucky I am. Between that and the book deal I got straight after graduation, it's practically a fairy tale."

"You're remarkably well-adjusted, and you have a good head on your shoulders when it comes to your work," he says, swirling the wine in his glass. "You didn't let it get to you, being such a smash hit."

"I know success can disappear"—I snap my fingers—"just like that. Especially in this industry. But more than that, the economy can take a turn, or a person can get sick. Life changes in ways we can't predict. I won't let today's success go to my head."

"I knew you were something special as soon as we met."

I know he means it in the nicest way possible, but that doesn't stop me from snorting. "When I was on my hands and knees in the hallway?

Wanting to cry but wanting to save myself from looking like even more of a mess?"

"You know what I mean." His hand finds mine just before he lifts it, pressing his lips to the backs of my fingers and basically turning me into a puddle of melted Kitty. "I knew you were the real deal."

This probably isn't the best time to remind him that he also thought I was only using him, so I keep that fun fact to myself and choose to revel in his sweetness. "I didn't know they made men like you anymore," I admit. It sounds corny as Kansas in springtime, but it's true.

"Like me? What's that mean?" he asks with a note of humor in his voice.

"Chivalrous and kind and thoughtful. You know what I'm trying to say. You're pretty special too."

"Even without the billions to my name?" He winks.

If he sounded even a tiny bit serious, it would turn my stomach. The fact that he's obviously making fun of himself and of what people typically think of him is the saving grace.

"Let's face it." I shrug with a smirk. "If you weren't who you are, there wouldn't have been any reason for us to meet each other. So, I guess I'll have to accept that you're fabulously wealthy and move on."

Our meals arrive and just in the nick of time. My stomach hasn't stopped rumbling since we walked through the door. Thick cuts of prime rib cooked medium-rare, creamed spinach, scalloped potatoes, roasted onions and mushrooms. Another bottle of wine, too, and a basket of steaming rolls.

"This looks fabulous, but what do you plan on eating?" I ask, and his laughter rings out in the otherwise quiet room.

"Another thing I like about you," he observes after a few minutes of gorging ourselves.

"What's that?"

"You don't shy away from eating on a date."

Well, why not tell me I'm acting like a pig?

I put my fork and knife down for the first time since I picked them up and touch my napkin to my mouth. "Sorry. I was so hungry."

"Oh, for God's sake, eat," he urges. "I was being sincere. Enjoy the food. I'm sure they worked hard on it, and I brought you here because it's one of my favorites. I hate few things more than watching a woman wish she could enjoy something but stopping herself anyway."

"How can you tell she's only wishing she could enjoy it?" I ask before spearing my steak again. *To hell with it.* I'm going to enjoy it, just like he thinks I should.

His mouth screws up in a smirk. "There's a longing in the eyes that's hard to miss. I see it a lot in people who hold themselves back from what they really want in life. It's a hunger that goes beyond the physical. I decided a long time ago that I didn't want to be that person. I don't want to wander through my life with that sort of hunger always gnawing at me, you know?"

"I admire that. I could learn something from you."

"I bet there are a lot of things you could learn from me," he murmurs.

And I suddenly get the feeling we're not talking about steak dinners and champagne lessons. The tingling sensation in my core tells me so along with the warmth spreading through me. Warmth that has nothing to do with wine.

It's a miracle I can even walk out of the restaurant by the time we're finished.

"Oof," I groan, laughing at myself. "My eyes were bigger than my stomach."

He must think I'm a total pig at this point, but I couldn't help it. Every forkful was better than the one before.

And let's face it; I had no idea if or when I'd ever be able to enjoy such an incredible meal again. A girl needs to take advantage of these opportunities.

"That's a shame since I was about to suggest we head to a jazz club I'm part-owner of." He sighs, clicking his tongue and shaking his head in mock dismay. "If you're too stuffed to go and do a little dancing and drinking ..."

"I think I can manage that," I blurt out, making him laugh as we reach the sidewalk.

"I thought you'd feel that way." He chuckles, turning to me.

His hands find my waist, and I don't shy away, not even when he pulls me a little closer. If anything, I've been dying for the opportunity to be this close to him, face-to-face, and my heart pounds hard enough that I have to wonder if he can hear it.

His eyes dart across my face. "Where did you come from, Kitty Valentine?" he whispers.

"Brooklyn, remember?"

"No, no. You must've come from another planet. They don't make women like you anymore."

"Funny. I was thinking the same thing about you earlier. Not that I think you're a woman or anything."

He laughs softly before lowering his head, hesitating for one soul-searing second before catching my mouth with his. He tastes like wine and the glass of scotch he finished the meal with—something my consciousness registers along with the strength of the arms he winds around my waist and the firmness of his chest. He crushes me against that chest when his arms tighten, and that's good since I need something to lean against when my legs go weak.

His mouth moves slowly over mine, nibbling and tasting, almost playful. Teasing me, tantalizing, making me stretch upward to reach him. What can I say? There are certain hungers that a steak dinner can't sate.

The only thing that could stop us at this moment would be the ringing of his cell, which is why the buzzing coming from his breast pocket comes as no surprise. Because of course, the phone would ring while I'm in the middle of being kissed like I've never been kissed before.

"Damn it," he growls, sliding a hand between us to reach for the device. "I'm sorry."

"It's okay," I breathe, dizzy and painfully aroused. This is the moment when I'm supposed to be the cool girl, right? The one who doesn't get flustered when her first kiss with somebody shaping up to be her dream man gets interrupted.

He's scowling when he answers the call. "Yes? Yes, I know. No. I'm in Chicago. I told you, I had plans," he says, looking at the ground. "What do you mean, the board wants to meet? On a Sunday? Since when? You're kidding." He turns away, muttering a colorful array of curses as whoever is on the other end of the call explains the situation.

I might as well not be standing here, still in front of the hotel, still a little off-kilter after our kiss. Maybe even more so now that I know our plans for the rest of the evening have been ruined. Nobody has to tell me so. I'm a pretty smart girl.

He shoves the phone into his pocket before turning back to me, apology written all over his face. "I'm so sorry. Does it make me too much of a jerk to ask for a rain check on our trip to the club?"

"Of course not. You have important things to

do." I'm trying to smile, but my heart's not in it. Not that I had my sights set on jazz and dancing—though the dancing could've been nice, come to think of it.

It's just that I can't help but wonder, as we make our way back to the hangar, how much of Blake's life is available to the woman in it, whoever she happens to be.

And whether that woman could ever be me.

Chapter Thirteen

"THIS WAS A good vintage—2008," Bryan informed her as he poured a glass of fizzy amber liquid. "I think you'll enjoy this."

Phoebe barely managed to suppress a smile. Like she would know the difference. But the least she could do was play along on this sudden detour to Chicago. "So long as we don't drink too much and miss tomorrow's presentations," she murmured, taking a flute from her boss's hand.

Was the brush of his fingers against hers an intentional thing? Was she a complete idiot for even asking herself such a question? *There was no way on earth the man was interested in her outside of their professional relationship.*

And no way he could know about the fantasies he inspired …

I roll my head on my neck and wonder if the greats ever questioned their writing the way I'm doing right now. It's just that I never had to think much while doing this before—not that writing was easy per se, but I was comfortable. Words flowed with ease.

I'm overthinking this.

Phoebe and her boss have to get something going on while flying either to or from Chicago. They just have to. They've been flirting and ratcheting up the tension for thousands of words. I doubt my readers, whoever they are, will feel like waiting much longer before a pulsing, throbbing cock pops out.

I wince at the thought. *How am I supposed to write about this when I can't even keep a straight face while thinking about it?*

What would he think if he knew how much sleep he'd cost her? Not to mention, productivity. How was she supposed to work when all she could think about lately was how much she wanted him to clear off her desk with a sweep of his arm and tear off her panties? Preferably with his teeth.

I can picture Blake that way. I can imagine him in all sorts of ways in fact.

Before I know it, my imagination starts running away with me. Sure, Blake with my underwear in his teeth. He spits them out—no! He buries his nose in them to inhale my scent before tossing them aside and burying his face in my—

"Damn it!" I growl when the phone rings. Just when I was starting to get into it. "This'd better be good," I warn Hayley on answering.

"Ouch. That's what I get for taking time out of my ridiculously busy day, huh?"

"It's Sunday. How busy can you be?"

"Hella busy, thanks very much." She sounds downright annoyed now, which saddens and chastises me.

"Sorry. I'm in a mood. You know I'm always glad when you find time to say hello." Though preferably not while I'm starting to feel more than a little turned on by the notion of my boss going down on me. While I'm on a desk with my skirt hiked up … and I really shouldn't be thinking about this while Hayley's on the phone.

"How did it go last night? You know I've been dying to know! Where did you go?"

The question brightens my mood. "Nowhere special. We took the jet to Chicago."

"What?"

"And had dinner in this ridiculously amazing restaurant that used to be a speakeasy Al Capone had spent time in. My eyes almost fell out of my head. Did you know there are restaurants without prices on the menu?" For some reason, I still can't get over this.

"Shut up! That's so cool! The speakeasy stuff, I mean. I can't believe he whisked you away like that! Then, what happened?"

There goes my mood. It lasted all of ten seconds. "Well, we were supposed to go to a jazz club he owns part of, which I think is just about the neatest thing ever, and I had the feeling he was going to take me to his apartment afterward. He has one there."

"Of course he does. Was there any, you know, sexy stuff?"

"I wish. We did kiss though. That was nice."

"Just nice?" She laughs.

"No. More than nice. It was exciting and hot and thrilling. Sweet though. He was respectful. He took his time too, which I think we can both agree is a plus."

"Mmm," she sighs. "I love long, slow kisses. I miss them."

"But he got a phone call. Business." I lean back in the chair and close my eyes, one curled fist against my forehead. "It brought the night to an end real fast."

"Oh no. So, no jazz? No hot sex?"

"No sex at all." I snicker. "We flew home. He was on his phone the whole time, typing messages and taking calls to prepare for this huge board meeting or whatever."

"And what did you do?"

"I took notes on my phone—the jet, the dinner, all of it. What was I supposed to do?" I ask when she giggles. "I might as well have not been there. He barely said a word to me. For a minute, I thought maybe he was angry with me for some reason. It was only when he apologized again before dropping me off at home that I knew he was mad at himself and the people who wanted the meeting."

"Aw, that's a shame. I'm sorry. But, hey! You got to fly on a private jet, and you know what it's like to have dinner at a restaurant with no prices on the menu. You can use that for your book, right?"

"I took a peek at the bill after it was delivered," I have to admit. "The meal was over six hundred bucks. I'm sure it meant nothing to him, but I almost yelped."

"Wow! You'll have to bring me along on your next date."

"If there is a next date. I mean, things ended pretty strangely. He was already dialing his assistant when he got back in the car. He didn't even walk me up to my apartment."

"That doesn't mean anything," she says, sounding like the Hayley I know and love. "He was distracted. But if that kiss was anything like you described, he'll be calling soon. Mark my words."

"I hope he does. Not just because I have a book on the line either."

"I didn't think that was all there was to it," she gently assures me. "You sound so excited when you talk about him. And you're not a user. That's the last word I'd use to describe you. It's clear that you like him a lot."

"I do. He's such a gentleman and drop-dead gorgeous. I mean, I can hardly think straight sometimes when we're together. I just wanna stare at him. And he's generous and thoughtful, and he's a real person at heart. A normal guy. Except for the whole having-to-drop-everything-for-business side of things."

"I guess that comes with the territory," she says. "He's a powerful man. There's probably a million pies he has a finger in."

"Wow. There's a pretty image."

"You know what I mean, you weirdo. He's got a bunch of business interests. There. Satisfied?"

"Yes, smarty-pants. And of course, I know what you mean."

"It probably takes him forever just to clear a few hours in his schedule to spend time with you."

"Which is exactly what I'm talking about! You're making it sound like I should be grateful for any little bit of time he can spare. And, yes, I am. I know he goes out of his way to spend time with me. But I want more than that. Is it wrong for me to want more?"

"More than a man with the money to do anything you want at the drop of a hat? No, really," she insists when I scoff. "Think about this. Anything you want would be yours. From what you're telling me about him, he wouldn't deny you anything."

"Except for himself, which is all I'd want in the end. He's more than just a fat wallet. And honestly, I don't know how I feel about you making it sound like that's all I should care about. Who do you think I am? Don't you know me better than that?"

"I already told you, I know you're not that person. Don't take it the wrong way, please."

"How else am I supposed to take it? I don't care that he's a billionaire. I care that he's himself. That's all."

"I think you're getting mixed up. You're not supposed to be dating him to fall in love or anything like that. You're supposed to be using him for research."

My mouth opens immediately, a cute little retort on the tip of my tongue. Only I can't go through with delivering it since she made a good point. I hate it when she makes a good point, especially when she's disagreeing with me.

"I know," I sigh instead of telling her off.

"But you can't help yourself, can you?"

"I wish I could. Maybe I can. I have to face this professionally, is all. I can't let him get to me. I mean, this is one book of many. I'll have to date a ton of guys to keep cranking out new books."

"Or … you could marry Blake and never have to worry about writing again!"

"Shut up!" I yelp, and we both laugh. "You're not helping."

"I know; I know. I couldn't help it. And don't pretend it wouldn't be amazing, being the wife of a billionaire."

It would be incredible. I know he would make it that way for me, for us.

But how many special evenings would end abruptly because of an unforeseen phone call? How many vacations would I spend alone because he couldn't get away from work?

Besides … "I wouldn't ever want to stop writing, you know."

"I know, but you could write what you want. You wouldn't have to worry about marketability or any of that."

"I thought you were a fan of me taking my career to the next level."

"I'm a fan of whatever makes you happy, sweetie."

And I know she means it, which is why I'm able to end our call with a smile.

"Okay," I whisper to myself, flexing my fingers. "Where were we? Oh, yes. Blake had his head between my thighs."

Amazing how easy it is to write a sexy scene when there's somebody in particular who you wish were doing those things to you …

Chapter Fourteen

"YOU HAVE NO idea how sorry I am."

"Really, it's okay!" I mean, it's not. But it is. "There was nothing you could do about it. You're a busy person. If anything, I felt sorry for you."

"Sorry for me?" Blake points to himself with a bemused expression, his mouth pulling downward at the corners. "Why would you feel sorry for me?"

Whoops. Maybe that was the wrong thing to say. After all, we're in his car, being driven to his penthouse here in the city—purely for research purposes, he's assured me multiple times. Now, it seems like I've insulted him.

Hopefully, he's enough of a gentleman not to push me out of a moving car.

"Don't get me wrong," I babble. Yes, I'm babbling, and my palms are all sweaty. "Not that you're pitiable or anything. I mean, you have it all—at least, it seems that way. Millions of people would kill to be in your shoes. Even the cheapest shoes you own."

He snorts softly, but his face is still an unreadable mask. A handsome, unreadable mask with just a touch of scruff on the cheeks. I wonder how that scruff would feel against the insides of my thighs, which is where Blake was all day—at least, in my fantasies, which are about all I have to work from right now.

"But I felt sorry for you anyway because you're always on call. It must be tough, trying to plan a special night or a vacation when there's no telling what's going to happen. So many people depend on you."

"They do," he sighs. "And no worries. I understood what you meant. I'm tired and a little cranky, is all."

"We don't have to do this, especially tonight. You probably just got back to town."

"I did." He rubs the back of his neck, grimacing like there's tightness in his muscles. "But I couldn't wait to see you again. Sometimes, I'm stubborn. And I wanted to make it up to you after cutting things off so suddenly last night."

Make it up to me? I catch my bottom lip under my teeth. "What do you have in mind?" I ask in what I hope is a cool, confident, worldly sort of way. So what if my palms are sweatier than ever? And oh, great, so are my underarms?

A slow smile spreads, and he doesn't look so tired anymore. "You'll see."

"Is it okay that I dressed casually? Like you said I should?" Granted, I'm more dressed up than I would be if I was hanging around the apartment, the way I normally do on a Sunday night. But still.

"You look gorgeous. And, yes, it's fine. We'll be staying in tonight."

How is it that the simplest, most innocent statement sets my heart racing? Who wouldn't want to stay in with him?

Preferably in bed. Naked. A little sweaty and breathless.

"How's the writing coming along?" he asks as we ride from the Upper East Side down into Midtown.

"Can you read my mind?"

"What's that mean?"

"It means, I've been imagining what else I can put in my book, based on what you've shown me so far."

"I won't take offense to that." He snickers. "Though I sort of wish you were fully with me and not halfway in your book."

"I'm not, really," I insist before putting my hands to my cheeks. They're hot to the touch, which doesn't come as a surprise. "I'm so embarrassed."

"Why?"

"Because ... oh jeez," I whisper, shaking my head. "It's too much. Let's just say, I need to write ... other things. In ... interesting locations ..."

He manages not to laugh at me. "Oh. You mean, sex? You have to write sex scenes, and you're trying to imagine doing it here, in the car?"

"No! Oh my God, I'm going to die of embarrassment. I shouldn't have said anything."

He catches my wrist, chuckling as he raises my hand to his lips. *Does he have any idea how sexy that is?* Just the slightest kiss on the back of my knuckles, and I'm putty in his large, capable-looking hands.

"If you want me to show you what it's like to play in the backseat of a moving car, I'm all yours. There's a privacy divider between the front and back for a reason."

Dear Lord, he's beautiful, and when he gets that little growl in his voice, he's practically irresistible.

There's no ignoring the tingling between my legs, where I spent the day imagining Blake firmly planted. For one wild, breathless moment, I want to tell him to raise that divider and put his hands on me, all over me. I'm tired of playing and hinting and fantasizing.

Still …

"Maybe we should start off a little slower," I suggest with a catch in my throat.

"That can be arranged too."

His lips linger on my skin again, and I forget to breathe when our eyes meet. Yes, I want this. I want him. Whenever, wherever—it doesn't matter.

It's probably for the best that we pull up in front of a tall building a few moments later.

I can hardly believe my eyes once I manage to pry them from Blake's. "You live on Fifth Avenue? In this building?"

"You're familiar with it?" he asks with a wry chuckle before climbing from the car.

I know by now that he'll jog around to my side and open the door for me. It gives me just a few seconds to compose myself.

Yes, I'm familiar with this building. It was refurbished several years back, and the apartments were snapped up in a flash by some of the biggest names in entertainment, tech, commerce. The penthouse, in particular, was famous for its asking price. More than seventy million dollars for over ten thousand square feet, not counting the expansive terrace overlooking the island.

I know before entering the private elevator that the penthouse is exactly where we're going.

"This is so beautiful," I marvel at the sleek marble floor, the rich, dark wood that panels the walls.

"It's the inside of an elevator car," he reminds me.

"When you were a kid back in Philly, did you ever imagine that you'd think nothing of a gorgeous elevator like this? That it would be commonplace?"

I can tell he's laughing at himself now. "You're right. Thank you for reminding me. Even I can become jaded."

The doors open, and suddenly, I'm staring at the inside of the most mind-blowing apartment I've ever seen. I saw photos when the place was up for sale; it was all over real estate news around the time I was searching for my apartment, and, well, a girl can dream.

But those photos were nothing compared to the real thing.

"Have a look around," Blake invites me as he walks across the wood floor, waving me in. "Are you hungry? I can order up anything you want. Anything at all."

It's hard to keep my mouth closed as I survey the room. The floor plan is almost completely open, the outer-facing walls mostly windows, which give a panoramic view of the city around us. There's a fireplace in the center, the living room furniture arranged in front of it. For such a sleek apartment, the furnishings are downright comfortable-looking. I can imagine getting cozy on the sofa, lost in a book.

"Hmm?" I ask when I find him staring at me, waiting. "Oh. Yeah. I could eat, sure. But please, whatever you want. You're the one who's been on the road all day."

"Do you like sushi?"

"I love it."

"Done." He pulls out his phone and types something in. "While we wait, I'd like to take a shower. Do you mind keeping yourself occupied for a few minutes?"

"Not at all." No, there's plenty to see all around me. "Take your time."

Maybe I watch a little too closely as he jogs up the stairs. What can I say? I admire the male figure, and he's worthy of admiration.

Boy, oh boy. How does anybody get anything done when they live in an apartment like this? I'd never stop looking out the windows. The city is laid out before me, no matter where I go, lights twinkling against the night sky. It's breathtaking, awe-inspiring. And to Blake, it's commonplace.

The sound of the shower rings out in the back of my mind, and I can hear him singing some tuneless little melody. I can't help but smile. He's a man of many talents.

Talents which, if I play my cards right, I'll have the chance to explore tonight. My heart just about beats out of my chest at the slightest thought of it, and I raise my hand to my lips to kiss the spot he kissed in the car.

"You can do this," I whisper to myself, shaking my hands out and bouncing up and down on the balls of my feet. "You can do this. You're a goddess. A wanton sex goddess. You're going to rock his world, Kitty Valentine. And you won't do it in missionary. You absolutely will not, under any circumstances. You'll be downright brazen. Like an animal finally released from a cage. He won't know which end is up by the time you're finished. He might need an IV or something to replenish himself."

I catch myself, freezing solid. *Blake is right behind me, isn't he? Of course he heard everything I just said because that's how my luck runs.*

Only he's not there. I'm alone, and he's still up-stairs. The shower has stopped, and there's no more singing, but he hasn't come down yet. Thank God for small favors.

A sudden buzzing makes me jump. My head sweeps back and forth as I try to figure out where the noise is coming from. In a moment, I realize it's the elevator, that somebody's coming up.

This is new. What am I supposed to do? I can't im-agine people randomly coming up on the elevator. *The front desk staff wouldn't allow that, would they?*

"Uh, Blake?" I call out, but there's no answer from upstairs. *When did this become an episode of* The Twilight Zone? *When did I become the last person on earth?*

Luckily, it's just one of the front desk personnel, carrying an overstuffed shopping bag in each hand. "Mr. Marlin's dinner order," the young man informs me, putting the bags on the floor just outside the elevator car.

"Oh, thank you," I breathe, laughing a little. "Sorry, he's up in the shower. Let me get you a tip."

"No need. Mr. Marlin makes sure everything's taken care of."

What a cryptic thing to say, and I have no choice but to shrug and accept it and thank the clerk again for taking the trip upstairs.

"Blake? Dinner's here." My voice echoes through the downstairs and, I'd guess, floats up to where my host is getting dressed. At least, I think he is. I haven't heard so much as a squeaky floor-board.

Finally, I can't help myself. I have to tiptoe up the stairs and see what I can see. "Yoo-hoo? Blake? Where'd you go?"

Just my luck, him having an accident while I'm downstairs, trying to talk myself into being a wanton sexual beast. He could've been bleeding out on the shower floor while I was trying to convince myself to try doggy-style.

Only he wasn't, and he's not now.

No, he's stretched out across the bed with a towel around his waist, feet still on the floor.

I'm not sure what's more interesting. Is it the king-size bed? The ultra-expensive workout equipment in one corner? The bathroom I can see through the open door with a soaking tub positioned right beside the window?

Or is it the man on the bed, the water still beading on his skin? The muscles—oh Lordy. His body is something I'd expect to see in a museum, carved out of marble. He could make a fortune as a fitness model if he ever got tired of being a media mogul.

Is that what I like the most? What has the breath catching in my throat?

No. It's the fact that he's fast asleep, snoring softly.

So much for rocking his world.

Chapter Fifteen

"HEY, BEAUTIFUL. WAKE up."

I don't wanna. It's so comfy here, on the sofa, propped up on what feels like a million pillows.

Crap. Blake's sofa. Blake's pillows. Blake's penthouse.

My eyes fly open a split second before I bolt upright, which is a real shame—that whole bolting thing—since Blake is leaning over me. Stars explode behind my eyes when our heads collide.

"Oof!" he groans, reeling backward with one hand over his forehead. "Wow. Remind me never to wake you up again."

"I'm sorry. I'm sorry," I babble, holding my head the way he's holding his. "I didn't know you were so close. I'm sorry."

"It's okay." He's grimacing though as he rubs where I smacked into him. "I should be the one apologizing to you after falling asleep. It's unforgivable."

"I wouldn't go that far." I grin. "You were exhausted."

He looks down at the sofa, where the book I was flipping through before falling asleep is still open.

"At least you found a way to keep yourself occupied."

"Your library is amazing."

And it is—floor-to-ceiling books along three walls. A bookworm's wet dream, in other words. Now, there's something I could write an erotic scene about, no problem.

"Thanks. I'm a big reader."

"I guess you have to be."

It's still dark outside, I note. "What time is it?"

"Just after ten. Neither of us slept very long. I really am sorry." He looks around. "I guess dinner's a no-go?"

"I put it in the fridge. It's only been a couple of hours. Do you think it's still good?"

"Only one way to find out. No, no, let me," he urges when I start to get up. "I'll bring it out to you. Wine?"

"Sure, thanks."

I manage to smooth out my hair and check my face for any dried spit or eye crusties or anything like that while he walks to the kitchen, barefoot. He's only wearing a pair of soft cotton pants. No shirt. The gods are smiling upon me.

Which is why looking like death warmed over after my little nap is a harrowing thought.

Soft jazz music starts coming from someplace, making me jump for the second time tonight. *Where the heck are the speakers?* I can't see them anywhere, but there's definitely a soft melody flowing through the living room when Blake brings me a glass of white wine, leaving the bottle and a second glass on the coffee table before scooting back to the kitchen.

"I figured we could still have some good music, like I was hoping to enjoy with you last night."

"This is nice." I smile over my shoulder, and it is. Better than nice. The sort of thing a girl could get used to without much effort.

"Just nice, huh?" He's smiling as he brings the food in, cartons stacked one on top of the other and tucked under his chin to keep everything from falling to the floor. "I'll have to try a lot harder then."

"Not that I would stop you"—I smirk—"but you know what I mean. If I called it extraordinary, I'd sound like an idiot. Even though it is."

"And you wouldn't. You're too hard on yourself. You've gotta stop that." He plops right down on the floor across from me and starts opening the containers. "I don't think you could sound like an idiot if you tried."

"Now, I know you're only trying to butter me up." I laugh. "You don't have to make up for falling asleep. I totally understand."

"You're tough." He hands me a pair of chopsticks—nice, shiny, not the sort a restaurant sends with their food. His own, I'd guess.

"Is this actual rose-gold gilding?" I ask, examining them. The wood looks like ebony too.

"Mmhmm. Not that it makes the food taste better or anything like that, but what the hell?" He sweeps his bare, muscular arms over the table, where an array of sushi, sashimi, and various rolls await. "Dig in. Let me recommend this roll right here." He points to a large, colorful one.

"What is it?"

"Spicy yellowtail, tempura shrimp, and banana."

"Stop it."

"I'm serious!" He takes a piece for himself, popping the whole thing in his mouth at once.

Judging by the way his eyes close, I'm guessing it's quite good. I also wonder what a girl has to do to put that look on his face because I sure would like to.

"Okay. I'll try anything once." I take a piece and manage to somehow fit it into my mouth. "Oh. Oh my."

"Right?"

"It shouldn't work, but it does!"

"I know. Crazy. Just goes to show you, don't judge a roll by its ingredients. Sometimes, everything works together and gives you something way better than the individual parts."

"You're a pretty smart guy." I take a piece of salmon sushi. The fish practically melts in my mouth, and the rice is perfectly seasoned. "This is incredible."

"I wish we could've eaten it when it was a little fresher. For future reference, you're more than welcome to wake me up when I fall asleep."

Future reference, huh? That bodes well. "I'll keep that in mind."

"Because a man would have to be out of his mind to make a mistake like that twice in a lifetime."

Our eyes meet, another piece of salmon on its way to my mouth. I pause with the chopsticks midair. "It wasn't that big a deal, you know," I whisper. "It's okay."

"A beautiful woman in my home, waiting for me downstairs? And I fall asleep? I could've kicked myself when I woke up. For a minute there, I thought you must've gotten tired of waiting and gone home."

"I wouldn't do that."

"You had every right to, but I'm glad you didn't."

"I didn't try to steal anything either, if you're worried about that."

He coughs hard, eyes bulging.

Great. I just killed one of the wealthiest men in the world before I even had the chance to get him into bed. "Sorry!"

He shakes his head. "No, it's okay," he manages to say once the sushi is out of his throat. "It's just that I never thought you did. The things you come up with."

"Are you kidding? If I were you, I'd always worry about somebody trying to steal from me."

"That's why I employ people I trust, who make sure such things won't happen." He takes another piece of that stellar banana roll and pretends like he's shooing my chopsticks away when I go for one too. "I said try it, not take all of it."

"Hilarious." I stick my tongue out at him before popping the strange, heavenly concoction in. "Gosh, that's good. This is all so nice."

"I'm glad I could manage to at least partly salvage what I've messed up." He puts down the chopsticks and looks at me from across the table, serious now. "I can't stop messing things up. It seems like, no matter how I try, something always goes wrong. I live a complicated life. There aren't many women willing to put up with the life I lead, the schedule I keep."

"I understand."

At least he sees it anyway.

"Yes, but understanding only runs so deep and only for so long. I find a woman I really like, somebody who makes me laugh and helps me stay grounded. She's beautiful and talented and smart. And all I can do is screw things up."

"I hope you're not talking about me because I don't think you've screwed up. Not even a little."

He's smiling softly as he rises from the floor in one fluid motion. His body is a work of art all right, and he moves with fluid grace. "Come here," he murmurs, holding a hand out.

I stand in front of him and put a hand on his

bare shoulder as he slides an arm around my waist. He takes my right hand in his, firmly clasping it and holding it between us. "I just have to dance with you. I've been wanting to for days, ever since I had the idea of taking you out this weekend."

Can he feel how fast my heart is racing as we sway back and forth, slowly and gently in time with the rich, sensuous piano coming from those invisible speakers? His skin is smooth and warm, and I want nothing more than to sink my fingers into the muscles of his shoulder. His mouth is close to my ear, his breath tickling my skin and bringing goose bumps up all over my neck.

"You're so beautiful," he whispers. "Not just physically—I mean, you're ravishing, but you're much more than that. I wonder if you'll ever figure out how special you are." His hand presses against my back, fingers working against the thin fabric of my blouse and just about undoing me.

My skin flushes hotter than before, about bursting into flames when his lips find my earlobe. My nerves are sizzling, my head spinning. *Is this really happening?* I wish there were something I could say, something clever or even seductive. I'm supposed to know so many words, right?

There's nothing I can say, nothing that would make any sense with everything rattling around in my overheated brain. I can only turn my head slightly, so my lips graze his chiseled jaw. He pulls his head back a fraction, putting us face-to-face.

God, I can't breathe. There might as well be nobody in the world but the two of us as we sway together, my body pressed against his. I'm falling, falling, but he catches me when our mouths meet.

There's no hesitation now, the arm around my waist tightening before lifting me off the floor. I instinctively wrap my legs around his waist, letting him carry me to the sofa where he sits with me in his lap.

"What about dinner?" I whisper as his mouth moves over my jaw, down my throat.

"We can order more," he growls before capturing my mouth again and doing things with his tongue that ought to be illegal, but I'm glad they're not because, oh jeez, I've never been kissed like this in my life.

Now, I can dig my fingers into his muscles, and thank heavens for that. I hold on to his shoulders for dear life, gripping him hard as my hips start moving on their own. He holds my hips, pulling down, driving his covered length against me while we make out like horny teenagers.

"Kitty ..." he groans before burying his face in my neck, breathing hard, kissing and tasting while I run my fingers through his hair.

This is wild, perfect, on the verge of being something truly great.

Until ...

I open my mouth.

And burp.

Loudly.

Like, there's some serious bass in it, and it echoes off all the hard surfaces in the penthouse until it sounds like a drunken longshoreman just passed through.

I freeze.

So does he.

I wanna die.

I don't realize until he starts shaking that he thinks this is funny. He's shaking with laughter which, bless his heart, he's trying so hard to hide but can't manage it.

"I'm sorry! Don't take it the wrong way!" he urges, tears rolling down his cheeks as my face burns with shame.

I tumble off his lap, horrified. "I'm so sorry. That was disgusting."

"It was normal." He chuckles, wiping his eyes. "Oh, Kitty, you're the whole package. It's my fault for getting things started while we were halfway through our meal. Don't be embarrassed," he insists when I don't crack a smile. "I've heard a lot worse. I've seen a lot worse too. You're a human being who just ate a bunch of sushi and drank some wine. It's not the end of the world."

No, but it's hardly the sexiest thing I've ever done either.

There goes the whole sex-goddess thing.

Chapter Sixteen

"HOW CAN YOU eat that?"

Matt looks up at me from the metal container he's currently digging through with his chopsticks. Definitely wooden, definitely the sort that come with the meal and have to be broken apart and rubbed free of splinters. Not a bit of gilded rose gold in sight. "Huh?"

I point to his food with my own plain chopsticks. "That."

"Chow mein?"

"It looks like something I once vomited."

"Oh, charming. That's definitely the sort of thing you should be talking about when a person's trying to eat." That doesn't stop him from digging back in—probably with more gusto than he actually feels, all in an effort to disgust me. "Let's not forget that I've seen you throw up, and it didn't look anything like this."

"You're gross."

"You started it."

He's right, of course, so all I do is stick my tongue out at him.

"Thanks for paying the delivery fee anyway."

"And now, you have the nerve to sit here and criticize my food choices." He shakes his head. "Ungrateful."

"That's just a drop in the bucket compared to what you owe me," I remind him before picking up a piece of sesame tofu.

"Meanwhile, how can you eat that garbage? It's like eating a sponge."

"No, it isn't."

"It is."

"When's the last time you ate tofu?"

He shrugs. "I don't remember."

"When's the last time you ate a sponge?"

"This morning."

I barely manage to keep a straight face. "You've probably never eaten tofu, and you're just parroting what you heard somebody else say."

Is he blushing? It could be a trick of the midday light flooding in through my living room windows. This is the first time Matt's ever been here. I just straightened up yesterday while avoiding a tricky plot point in Phoebe's story, so I figured it was safe to have him over. No random underwear or feminine hygiene product wrappers in the bathroom—that sort of thing.

"Have I ever talked about my best friend, Hayley?" I ask. It's a question I didn't plan on asking. I'm just as surprised as he is at the sound of it coming from my mouth.

He frowns, lowering the white container of rice he was just shoveling in. "I don't think so. Why?"

"She had a super-embarrassing thing happen the other night, and I told her it's probably more common than she thinks it is." Okay, bald-faced lie. That's what Hayley told me when I texted her—that it was common for people to let loose with various bodily noises, even when they were making out or in the middle of having sex.

Am I as sheltered and prudish as everybody's been accusing me of lately? Because it's starting to seem that way.

"Oh?" He goes back to shoveling rice in like it's his job. "What happened?"

I can tell he doesn't really care, and that's probably not a bad thing. No sense in him paying close attention. This isn't supposed to be anything deeper than idle conversation.

"She was making out with some guy, and it was getting pretty hot, you know. But then she burped. Like, loudly."

He snorts. "That sucks."

"I know. She was so humiliated. She doesn't know whether the guy will want to see her again or anything."

His eyes meet mine for a beat when he glances up from his food. "Hmm."

"Hmm?"

"Is it that big a deal? Burping? I mean, I could burp for you right now, if you want."

"I don't want."

"I'm just saying."

"Yeah, I know you are, but why would I want you to?"

He shrugs. "It's a normal thing."

"For a guy maybe. Not for a girl. We're not supposed to do things like that."

"That's dumb."

"I don't make the rules. That's what we're raised to believe. No burping. No …" I wave my hand around behind me, near my butt. "Only in private."

"Is that why I've never heard that from anybody I've dated? I thought they all had something wrong with them."

"Stop it."

"I'm serious." He looks it too. "I didn't know it was, like, social conditioning."

"Are you truly that obtuse?"

"Now, you're just being hurtful." But he's grinning, so I figure it doesn't bother him too much. "So, what did your date think when you burped in front of him?"

"He said it was okay—" My chopsticks clatter to the floor once I stop talking because, dang it, he got me.

And he loves it.

"I thought so." He laughs. "You're not a good liar. You suck at it, in fact."

"Laugh all you want," I mutter, teeth clenched. "It was a very real embarrassment for me. But please, take pleasure in my humiliation."

"I doubt it was that humiliating."

"What did I just tell you? It's unladylike and gross."

"If you think a burp is the least ladylike thing there is, you must be a miserable lay."

"Hey!" I grab the closest thing to me—a packet of duck sauce—and fling it his way. "That's rude and wrong. I'm not a miserable lay."

"Do you ever make noises?"

"That's not the same as moaning somebody's name, Matt."

"Ooh. Say it again. My name. But moan it."

"Shut up."

He sits back in his chair, crossing one bare ankle over the other knee. He truly doesn't like wearing shoes. Even in my apartment. I guess it's okay. I threw up all over his place after all, and I've slept naked in his bed.

"Okay. Serious now. What did your date say or do when you were so unladylike?"

I don't know what's more humiliating—having gone through it or having to tell the story to this smirking, smug jerk. I shouldn't have said a word. "He laughed until he cried."

A twitch of his lips. "At you? Or at the situation?"

"What's the difference?"

"Did he point at you and laugh and ask why you even bother breathing, being such a pig?"

"No!"

"So, he laughed because it was funny and unexpected, and you should've laughed with him and gotten past it instead of making it a big deal. I'm guessing that's what you did."

I wish I could tell him he was wrong. I really do. "I was embarrassed."

"Everybody does embarrassing things sometimes. I guess when you're, you know, in a relationship or whatever, stuff's gonna happen. I wouldn't know, but I'm guessing." He pokes around his container, shrugging.

"You've never been in a relationship?"

"Not really."

I lean forward because this is intriguing. "No? You're sort of a catch. I mean, for a certain type of person who doesn't mind getting made fun of."

He points to himself, his lips pursed like he's surprised. "How am I a catch?"

"Don't make me throw anything else at you. You make decent money—at least, I guess you do. You're not completely heinous to look at." Massive understatement, but his ego is already inflated enough. "And you have a super-awesome neighbor who lives across the hall."

"Oh, I'm sure that would be a huge selling point." He rolls his eyes, snickering. "I guess I'm not cut out for it. Relationships. Commitment."

"No? You don't want to settle down with somebody? Make a life with them?"

"Not really." When I gape at him, he frowns. "What? Is that a crime?"

"No, not a crime. I just don't get it."

"You don't have to. It's my life. It's how I feel. Just because you believe in happily ever after doesn't mean the rest of us do or even want to. I'm happy enough by myself. I don't need anybody else to make my life happy or, you know, complete me."

"I never said I did either."

"No?" His brows lift, practically hidden under his floppy hair. "You write about that sort of stuff though. Don't tell me you don't believe in it."

"I do, but I don't need it."

"Right. You mean to tell me, if Mr. Wonderful proposed tomorrow, you wouldn't jump at the chance?"

"Blake would never do that, and I don't want him to. I hardly know him."

"I didn't mean him in particular. Just, you know, the perfect man for you. Hell, I sat here and told you I don't believe in settling down and building a life with just one woman, and your jaw hit the floor. Come on."

"You know what?" I stand, food forgotten. "You can leave my apartment if this is how you're going to be. I don't feel like having you criticize me anymore."

"I'm criticizing you? You're the one who acted like there's something wrong with me."

He stands, which I wish he hadn't done since

he's so much taller than I am. I don't like looking up at him.

With my chest stuck out and my hands on my hips, I snap, "You have commitment issues. That's not exactly healthy."

He points a finger at me. "And you're lost in some dream world where there's one person for everybody and nobody can make a life for himself or herself without having that one special person next to them. Where nobody wants to be single for the sake of being single. This is the real world, sweetheart, and some people just want to have fun. Not everything has to be so emotional."

"Get your finger out of my face and then get out of here," I growl, teeth clenched. "I don't appreciate your attitude."

"I don't appreciate yours."

"Go."

He does but not without slamming the door. I'm sorry he did because I wanted to be the one to slam it.

Chapter Seventeen

IT'S NOT ANOTHER two full days before I'm called upon to prove that I'm actually working on a new book, chock-full of sexy goodness. Or badness. Depending on how you look at it.

"Maggie," I chirp on answering her call. *Do I sound happy to hear from her? Dismayed? Desperate? Suicidal?* I can't tell.

And it's not like she cares very much either way. "How's the new book coming along?"

It's unlike her to call me while I'm in the process of writing something, which tells me she doesn't have a ton of confidence in what I'm doing. That's okay since I don't have a ton of confidence either.

"It's definitely coming along. I have a strong story, great characters. My heroine, Phoebe, is sort of a smart-mouth, and her boss likes that—"

"Great, great, but is it filthy? Oral? Anal? Bondage?"

My skin crawls. "It's pretty filthy. Lots of sex, lots of fantasizing before the sex happens. Her fantasies are pretty raunchy."

"Excellent. When do I get to see some of it?"

Yep, she's worried.

I stare at the blank page in front of me. There are plenty of pages filled with words on my computer, but this one happens to be empty. Because it's the page on which I have to start the big, important first sex scene between Phoebe and her boss. No more fantasies, no more flirting. They're on the jet, flying back from the weekend conference after Phoebe helped him pull off a major victory at the last-minute meeting.

So, they're celebrating, and soon, they will do so by inserting Tab A into Slot B. Only in a much sexier way. I hope.

"Uh, I can send you a bunch of chapters tomorrow morning, if that's okay? I wanna look through them before sending them over."

"Sure, that sounds great. I expect to need a fresh pair of panties by the time I'm finished reading."

Welp then. That doesn't nauseate me or anything. "I can only hope so," I manage to say before I have to end the call. I don't want to imagine how much worse this conversation could go.

Terrific. Now, I have to write a truly dirty, filthy, panty-flooding scene. And I have an entire day to do it.

The light outside my window changes as hours pass, and my fingers move much slower over the keys than I would like. Here's the thing about writing sex: everybody thinks it'll be easy until they have to sit down and do it themselves. It takes a strong imagination and the ability to see everything, from every angle, and describe it clearly.

But it has to be more than a bunch of body parts thrashing around. The best sex involves the feelings and thoughts and sensations the characters are experiencing. Otherwise, it might as well be a description written in a medical text.

Not sexy.

"I need to thank you," he murmured, his breath hot on Phoebe's already-overheated cheeks. "I wouldn't have been able to do that without you. You're a superstar."

If his nearness and the champagne hadn't already made her flush, she would've blushed to the roots of her hair. He was so close, closer than they'd ever been. The only time she'd ever been near enough to feel his breath on her face was in her daydreams and fantasies, and those didn't count.

"I did my job. It's what you pay me for." She shrugged. "Though a bonus wouldn't be out of the question."

"You think I should give you something extra?" A faint smile played over his generous mouth.

"I do."

"What if I don't have any extra cash to give you?"

She couldn't help but snicker softly. "You? No extra cash?"

"Not on hand. I'm afraid I'd have to come up with some other way to balance our accounts."

His gaze dropped to her chest, where she knew her V-cut neckline revealed more than she normally did at the office. Especially when leaning forward, the way she was now.

Instead of sitting up straight or adjusting the way the dress fell, she stayed just where she was and let him get an eyeful. The tip of his tongue moistening his lips just about undid her along with his deepening breath.

He wanted her. He wanted her just like she wanted him.

The touch of his hand on her knee only made her more certain.

"Sure, sure, that's right," I whisper, nodding slowly.

They're in the cabin of the jet, which, naturally, looks a heck of a lot like Blake's jet. My hero looks a lot like Blake Marlin, too, except his hair is jet-black and his eyes are like two chips of ice.

The similarities are a coincidence, of course. That's my story, and I'm sticking to it.

She slid over the buttery-soft leather, inching closer to him. Leaning into his touch. Letting his hand slide higher up her leg, setting her skin on fire with each skillful sweep of his fingers.

"I've been wanting to touch these legs of yours for as long as I can remember," he whispered, staring deep into her eyes.

"Really?" Not sexy or seductive. Surprised more like. "Me? You've been thinking about me?"

"Every morning," he confessed. "Every afternoon. Every night. You bend over a desk or lean in to look, and

I smell your perfume and your skin. When I feel your tits pressing against my shoulder or I see your ass stretching your skirt, it's all I can do to keep from taking you by the waist and …"

She shuddered as his fingers slid against the hem of her panties—panties which were getting more soaked by the second. Each word out of his mouth came out at once, in a single breath.

Hmm. Not bad. I managed to work wet panties into it and everything.

It's dark out now. I check the time and recoil when I see it's past midnight. *How did that happen? I never ate dinner. What was lunch? Did I eat that?*

This is the way it always goes when my back's to the wall, and I have no choice but to grit my teeth and get the work done. I lose track of time while typing, backspacing, typing, backspacing again, staring off into space and questioning my choice of career.

There's leftover curry in the fridge and enough greens for a salad to go with it. I've been shamefully lax with my eating lately, between gorging myself with Blake and noshing on leftover Chinese from my disastrous lunch with Matt a couple of days ago.

The thought of him is enough to boil my blood. *Obnoxious jerk. Talking to me like there's something wrong with me, and why? Because I believe in love and commitment? What's so bad about those things? Maybe if he had a good woman in his life, she'd take him down a peg or two and even out that inflated ego of his.*

Which is probably just as much a reason as any for him to stay single. He wouldn't want anybody to call him out on his stupidity.

I have bigger fish to fry. I can't afford to waste time thinking about him. Life was a lot easier back before we ever spoke a word to each other. Maybe I knew instinctively that he wasn't worth the time.

Now, he's in my head. I can't help but wonder why Blake hasn't called or texted all week, and I keep going back to what that idiot across the hall said. That I should've rolled with it, laughed it off, and gotten back to business.

I'm wondering if I lost that chance for good, all because I was ashamed of myself. I wish I could go back. I'd do it all differently. And I might even end up spending the night in Blake's bed, in Blake's apartment. In Blake's arms.

"Kitty Valentine, you need to grow up," I sigh, taking the curry off the burner and pouring it over the rice I heated up in the microwave. It's still tasty, and my stomach's glad to have something in it. I might think better with food in my belly.

Do I need to grow up? I guess so. No matter how I look at it, facts are facts. I've been sheltered, in a bubble. There's a reason Hayley encouraged me to date around. I have no experiences—not just sexual ones, but life experiences too. Like how to deal with embarrassing moments without making them worse.

It could be that I'm in the right business but the

wrong genre. I could write a how-to manual on how to deal with humiliation. Lord knows, I have enough personal experience to draw from.

Except I'd still have to learn how to deal with these situations without shriveling up and wishing I could die on the spot, so …

Back to writing sex. Imagining Blake in the position of the boss is helpful indeed. I can see him on the jet, can imagine him lowering himself to his knees in front of me. Taking my hips and jerking them until I'm at the edge of the chair, sliding my panties down, down, down …

Giggling in the hallway breaks my train of thought, and it's all I can do to keep from screaming. It's like the entire world is conspiring to keep me from writing this scene.

Matt's door opens and closes.

Wonderful. He's getting lucky tonight.

"Blake. Think about Blake."

I do that, turning my focus back to the jet cabin and Blake, on his knees, working my dress up to my hips and spreading my legs wide. My mouth goes dry as sand.

He inhaled her, eyes closing like he smelled the sweetest perfume. "Beautiful," he groaned before pressing his lips to her inner thigh. "So beautiful. So sweet. I need to taste you. I wanna lick you until you flood my mouth. Until you scream my name."

Phoebe shuddered in pleasure, the heady pleasure of knowing she was wanted. Watching this powerful man, this titan, on his knees and just about salivating at the scent of her …

"Do I have to use this word?" I whisper, frowning. *I guess I do. Maggie wants filth.* "P-U-S-S-Y," I mutter with each letter.

What would I do? How would I feel? Jeez, I could be taking this from a real-life memory if I hadn't been such an idiot before. I might not have to imagine what it would be like for Blake to go down on me if I hadn't ruined everything.

"Ooh … yeah …"

I look from the screen to the wall in front of me. *Did I imagine that? Is my fantasy that strong?*

Nope. No such luck. It's the lucky girl of the night, moaning like she's in the throes of bliss.

"Perfect timing," I mutter.

Phoebe closed her eyes, letting herself go. Letting him slide his tongue up and down the length of her cleft.

Is that the right word? Well, if Maggie doesn't like it, she can change it.

Letting him dip deeper, urging him to, she lifted her hips to meet his hungry tongue. "Please," she whimpered, forgetting to be shy or hesitant. How could she be hesitant when he was driving her crazy?

"Please what?" he growled before taking another lick and then another.

"Please … more. Harder. Make me come, boss."

"Oh, Matt! Baby, yes!"

"Give me a break," I mutter, rolling my eyes and pushing back from the desk in frustration.

At least she knows his name, but she sounds like she's practicing for a porn video. A really bad one where you know the girl is faking.

I've done a little research since that unfortunate incident with the volume control. I know what I'm talking about.

"Oh! Oh! Oh!" It's in time with what I guess is his thrusting or her thrusting onto him.

What is this man packing that he inspires that sort of squealing? Oh, right. I've pretty much seen it—at least, when it was tenting the front of his boxers and making me blush from head to toe.

I guess I'd sound like that too, if I were her. Though I'd at least put my face in a pillow or something. I'm not a complete barbarian.

Knowing him, he'd tell me not to. He'd take the pillow away because he'd want everybody to hear what he was doing to me.

I narrow my eyes and stare at the wall between our rooms. *How much would it cost to invest in a little soundproofing?* I might even be able to write it off as a business expense since there's no way I can concentrate when somebody's getting plowed next door.

A deeper voice joins hers. "Ugh! Yeah!"

Oh my Lord, he's grunting now. I wish my imagination weren't as good as it is. As strong as it is and as vivid. Because now, I'm imagining him slamming into this faceless girl for all he's worth, and it's killing me.

Which is what leads me to type a few words into my browser's search, and before long, rousing marching band music comes blaring from my laptop.

"See if this helps you maintain the mood." I grin, cranking up the volume until my ears are ringing.

No way he can't hear this. No way she can't. I don't care if she's on the verge of an earth-shattering orgasm.

I'd bet good money she's not anymore. Not with John Philip Sousa providing background music. I might have to put a playlist together.

After the third repeat of "The Stars and Stripes Forever," I let the music wind down. Nothing but silence reaches me after that.

Except for something that sounds like a fist hitting the wall. Just once, just hard enough for me to hear it.

But enough to let me know the message was received.

Chapter Eighteen

"YOU GOT TICKETS? Are you serious?" I'm holding a pair of tickets in my hand, sitting next to Blake in the backseat of his sleek car. A pair of tickets that most people can't get their hands on unless they're willing to give up a kidney. At least.

"Sure." He chuckles, kissing my cheek. "No problem. I thought you might be interested in seeing it."

"The entire world wants to see it." I turn to him, beaming. "I just can't wrap my head around this, is all. I didn't even think you wanted to see me again."

"Do me a favor and stop thinking that, right this very minute," he murmurs, closing one hand over my knee and stroking gently. "I've thought about you a lot. That's saying something, considering that I was on the road all week."

I settle back against the arm he's extended across the top of the seat, and he closes it around me. *This is nice. So nice.* I've been thinking about him, too, after all.

What would he think if he knew exactly what sort of thoughts he's inspired in my surprisingly dirty mind lately?

"Where were you?" I ask, breathing in the spicy scent of his cologne.

"Miami. LA. Up to Boston from there. And now, here I am."

"You must be exhausted."

"What, afraid I'll fall asleep on you again?" he asks with a playful smile before planting one sweet, lingering kiss on my upturned mouth.

No, that is certainly not what I'm afraid of. That's not what had me spending the day avoiding anything carbonated once I knew he wanted to go out tonight. Considering all the trouble I went to, getting myself ready—all those extra, above-and-beyond things a girl does for a special date—I don't want to do anything to spoil it.

"After this," he murmurs in my ear, tickling me with his breath, "I thought we could grab a late supper. My place maybe? If that doesn't suit you, I'm sure we can get in just about anywhere."

"Just by using your name?" I tease, and I get a kiss on the nose for it. "Your place sounds fine. I like the idea of having you all to myself."

He smiles, and his hand moves up my leg. "Funny. I was thinking along the same lines."

"Were you?" My gaze lands on the privacy glass separating us from the driver as my pulse picks up speed.

"Hmm." He kisses my cheek, my throat. "What are you thinking about, huh?"

I gasp when his hand reaches my upper thigh, fingers just barely skimming my skin. Amazing, how such a simple touch can set a person on fire. Here I am, dressed to the nines, having spent a solid hour on my hair and makeup, yet I'm already writhing against him.

"This is all I wanted when I was with you at my place," he whispers in my ear, his voice sultry. "To hear your reaction to being touched. To see you. To taste your skin. To make you feel good."

He's succeeding.

"Can I touch you?" he asks. "Can I make you feel good?"

"Oh, please do," I beg in the faintest whisper. I grip the seat when his fingers find my panties and then slide underneath to where it's so hot and slippery and aching. "Bl-Blake!" I gasp against his throat, drowning in his scent and his warmth and wave after wave of excruciating pleasure as he works my most private places until I'm on fire.

"That's right," he whispers. "Let go for me. Just for me."

That does it. I stiffen against him with a single soft cry that I sincerely hope the driver didn't hear before melting against Blake's firm chest and shoulder.

"Oh gosh," I breathe, chest heaving.

"So sweet," he whispers, kissing my temple and my forehead over and over. "So sweet."

"I can't believe that just happened," I confess

with a choked giggle.

"It definitely did. You deserve to feel that way all the time."

He watches as I straighten myself out, smoothing down my dress and my hair. I can hardly look at him, caught between embarrassment and giddy excitement and—let's face it—an afterglow.

We're at the theater a few minutes later, and I wonder if everybody around us knows something just happened in the car. How can they not know? I mean, it was one of the best orgasms of my life; it's got to be written on my face. But aside from a handful of people looking at Blake like they recognize him and a few handshakes and brief pleasantries with people I've never seen before, we don't make a big impression.

We have box seats, practically up against the stage.

"I can't believe this," I whisper for probably the tenth time as we sit. "I mean, this is extraordinary. Do you know how extraordinary this is?"

"I do." He grins before kissing me. "Certain things aren't lost on me, even now." He takes my hand just as the lights go down, and the murmuring throughout the jam-packed theater quiets.

What would it be like to live like this always? I can't help but imagine it as the show starts up and Blake's hand is still in mine. Box seats, the two of us holding hands after a little fun in the backseat of the car. I still feel giddy and like I could start giggling at any second.

I mean, is this my life? What did I do to get so lucky?

The first act is winding down by the time I lean over to whisper that very question into Blake's ear—only a certain buzzing from his jacket pocket interrupts me. He mutters a curse, which the rousing music drowns out.

I've gotta take this, he mouths, standing and slipping out of our box before the curtain falls.

Well, now's as good a time as any, I guess. Intermission is supposed to be fifteen minutes long. I'm too busy rushing to the ladies' room to worry much about it anyway.

Only once I'm finished and back in my seat, Blake's still nowhere to be found. I didn't see him in the lobby or the hall or by the bar where so many people were crowded between acts. My heart starts racing as disappointment spreads through me. I'd hate to see him miss any of the next act.

Or the first song. Or the second song.

Eventually, I have to give up hope of him coming back at all. I don't think he left me stranded here—heck, even if he did, I could find my way home. I'm a big girl. But I doubt he would've left without saying anything.

Though honestly, who knows? I would never have imagined him skipping out on the second half of the hottest Broadway musical of the last decade either, but here we are.

He's waiting by the car, pacing with his hands

in his pockets. "I'm so sorry," he says once I reach him. "There was nothing I could do. Did you like the show?"

"Sure." I shrug. "It was fantastic. I wish you could've seen it."

"Yeah. Me too." Blake helps me into the car and follows behind after telling the driver to go to his penthouse. He's short, curt. Angry about something.

Is it more than missing half the show?

"Is everything okay?" I whisper, closing a hand over his. I want him to know I'm with him. "You don't have to keep everything to yourself. If you need to talk, I'd love to listen."

I try not to take it personally when he snickers. "It's complicated. Business."

"Of course. I wouldn't expect anything else."

"What's that mean?"

Probably not the nicest thing I could've said, but I don't feel nice anymore. I feel ignored and lonely. "It means, you're always busy with business. And it puts you in a bad mood more often than not."

"That's not true."

"Almost every time we've been together, something has happened. A phone call, a last-minute meeting, you falling asleep because you're so tired from all this travel you're always doing. Don't get me wrong," I add when his mouth falls open. "I understand. But I don't have to be thrilled about it. I sat through the entire second half of the show by myself."

"You're not the one who had to miss half of it."

"No, but the whole time, I was thinking about how sad it was for you that you had to. You spent all the money on the seats—"

"The money," he scoffs, waving a hand.

"Yeah, I know. It means nothing to you. All these grand gestures that mean so much to me don't mean anything to you. You didn't get to see the second half of the show? No big deal. You'll get tickets for another performance. It doesn't matter that regular people can't get their hands on any. You can call somebody, and—poof—whatever you want is provided."

"What's so wrong with that?"

"What's wrong with it is … well, you won't get the chance to take me again. To sit with me and watch with me and hold my hand, the way you did at first. We were experiencing it together. That was better than box seats to any show imaginable. Being with you. Seeing it together. That mattered. Until it didn't."

Until I didn't. I won't say it. I can't say it. I'd never forgive myself for putting it all out there like that. For sounding needy and grasping and desperate.

Even if I feel more than a little needy right now.

"I hate to tell you this, but there's a price for the sort of lifestyle you just described, and it goes beyond the monetary," he mutters, looking out the window on his side of the car. "I told you that before. People think just because you're supposedly set for life, there's nothing else that needs to happen. You can sit right back and coast. That isn't the case."

Right. Now, I remember what he told me before, about dating girls who don't understand ambition and work ethic and whatever.

"Is this what you meant? That you don't like having somebody in your life who holds you accountable? Because I know what it means to work hard. I spend entire days in front of my computer. But I know there has to be balance too. Maybe it's time to take a step back and see what can be handled by other people."

"Oh. Is that what you think?" He turns back toward me, and I wish he hadn't since the hard look in his eyes makes me anything but comfortable. "I'm so glad to hear you have all the answers. Maybe you're the one who should be in my place."

"Okay, okay," I sigh.

"No, really. I mean, I've only managed to amass a billion-dollar fortune on my own. At a young age. When everybody I met thought I was out of my mind for dreaming as big as I did. I've managed to grow my holdings every year. Every single one. But please, tell me what you know about business since your career as a romance writer has given you so much insight."

It's like pouring alcohol onto a paper cut. His

words burn. His words and the tone behind them. The nastiness. Like the Blake I'm unfortunately falling for is one side of the coin, and this guy— hard, cold, sharp—is the other.

"I want to go home," I whisper, wrapping my arms around myself and turning away from him. "Now, please."

His sigh is heavy. *Is it regretful?* It should be, in my humble opinion, but that's just me.

"Don't do that. I'm—"

"You're a jerk," I whisper. It comes out thick, choked with tears, but I mean it. "And I want to go home. If you think this is gonna end well tonight, like I'll forget how nasty you just were and fall into bed with you, you're wrong."

He sighs again but taps against the privacy glass before touching a button to move it aside and give the driver new instructions.

We don't exchange another word the entire length of the ride, and he doesn't walk me to my door. I don't want him to. It wouldn't matter if I never saw him again.

THIS ATTITUDE LASTS until morning, when the scent of roses reaches me the moment I step into the living room. There aren't any flowers in the apartment, not anywhere. *Am I having a stroke?* No, roses aren't one of the things people smell when that happens—at least, so I've been told.

Why am I tiptoeing to the door? I have no idea.

Something weird is going on, and people tiptoe when weird stuff happens.

"You're kidding," I whisper once I open the door a crack and peer out into the hall.

It looks like someone replaced the plain wood floor with flowers. Lush, fragrant red roses, to be specific.

The hallway is full of them, bouquets and bouquets of the same enormous roses Blake gave me on our first date. They blanket the floor from wall to wall. There's no card, no message, but I don't need one.

The man knows he was wrong, and he knows how to make a gesture.

"Who died?"

My jaw juts out as I look from the flowers to Matt, who just opened his door. Leave it to him to ruin a nice moment like this, when I'm standing here with my heart swelling and one hand against my forehead.

"Nobody died."

"Because it looks like a funeral parlor out here." He sniffs and then wrinkles his nose. "Smells like one too."

"By all means"—I smile—"feel free to drop dead at any time, so the flowers can get some good use."

He only sighs before closing the door louder than he needs to.

Chapter Nineteen

"WHAT DID YOU do with all the flowers? Don't tell me they're in your apartment," Haley says.

"Gosh, no." I laugh before sipping my latte. "No, I packed them up in boxes and ordered up a big car and took them to the hospital."

"You didn't." Hayley's mouth hangs open.

"Why not? I figured people there would get a little happiness. What? Was I supposed to leave them to rot in my place?"

"No. I don't even know why I'm surprised," she admits with a warm smile. "That's exactly the sort of thing you would think to do."

I don't think it's that big a deal, honestly, but she seems to. I shrug it off. "Anyway, I kept a few bouquets for me. One in the living room, one in the bedroom, one on the counter in the bathroom. They're so pretty, and the whole apartment smells like them now." Better than smelling like reheated curry or whatever I most recently ordered to eat.

"He obviously regrets what happened," Hayley muses, watching me like a hawk.

I can feel her eyes boring holes into me, even

when I'm not looking. That's what years of super-close friendship does. A girl develops a sixth sense.

"Do I have something hanging out of my nose?" I finally have to ask. "Because you're staring at me."

"Oh, am I?" she asks with a smirk.

"You are, and you know you are."

"I only want to see how you feel about what's happening." She shrugs, flipping her impossibly silky hair over one shoulder. I swear, the girl looks like she stepped out of a shampoo ad. Or maybe an ad for a spa or salon. "You've been more tight-lipped than usual about him."

"There's not much to say. I told you what happened." Even the part in the car, which makes me blush, just thinking about it. "I mean, it's not even Sunday afternoon yet. Give me a chance to get everything straight in my head."

"You're being evasive."

"You're being impossible."

"Point taken, but you're still being evasive. Listen," she insists when I roll my eyes skyward, "I know you're developing feelings for him, but I could tell from the tone of your voice that it hurt you. He hurt you."

"We had an argument. He was a jerk about it. So was I though. I shouldn't have—"

"No, you had every right to." She sits back, arms folded, her jaw tightening the way mine does when I'm good and ticked off. "Just because he's richer than God doesn't mean his life is automatically more important than yours or anybody else's. And if he can't draw a line between work and his private life, that's his problem. It shouldn't have to be yours. You don't have to accept whatever little crumbs he throws your way just because he's an epic catch."

"Wow. Tell me how you really feel."

"I'm pissed on your behalf. I can't help it."

"I love you for it. But aren't you the one who told me just, what was it, a week ago, that this is the sort of thing to expect from somebody in his position?"

She rolls her eyes. "Yeah, yeah. I'm not always right. You should know that by now."

"I have to remember we're not actually dating." I look down at my plate, the half-eaten eggs Benedict staring back at me. Even after a morning spent delivering flowers, I don't have much of an appetite. I'm too conflicted.

"But you are. Even though the two of you walked into this with an understanding of why you'd wanted to approach him in the first place, you're dating. You've gone out, what, three times? And spent the night in once?"

"So what?"

"And there are feelings involved. Don't pretend there aren't," she murmurs, and I hate how sympathetic she sounds. "You like him. A lot. And it sounds like he likes you a lot too. It would be one thing if this was just for fun."

"Like Matt and his screaming banshees." I snicker.

"Exactly. But it's not. He's very sweet to you and tender and all that good stuff neither of us has had in our lives for way too long. I mean, you were bound to fall for him. I'd have been worried about you if you hadn't, quite frankly. I'd have had to check your pulse."

That gets a giggle from me anyway. "I don't have an excuse. I knew walking into this who I was dealing with. The sort of man he is, I mean. How busy and important he is. I can't complain now."

"You weren't complaining last night—unless there's something you aren't telling me."

"I told you practically the whole conversation, word for word."

"You were pointing out how wrong he was, and you had every right to," she decides with a firm nod. "And you're absolutely right. Having a strong work ethic is one thing, but he lets work consume him. No wonder he has such a hard time with relationships. I mean, I can't imagine I'd be much better if I were in his shoes—though I'd like to try." She grins, eyebrows wiggling up and down.

I raise my latte in her direction. "Amen to that. Though I don't know if I'd want to live his life."

"No?"

I shake my head. "I mean, okay, I'm what you'd call a successful author."

"Putting it mildly."

"I don't feel comfortable calling myself a current success. Anyway, I still get to be anonymous— mostly. I don't have to worry about going out in public and being recognized. Meanwhile, Blake goes to a restaurant or a show, and he's got to deal with people looking at him. He has to wonder if anybody's going to approach him or bother him or take pictures. He doesn't say it out loud, but I can tell how guarded he feels. Tense, eyes always sweeping the room. He wants to pretend to be normal when he's anything but. I wouldn't want that."

"Understood."

"And for somebody whose fabulous, healthy lifestyle is held up as some great example, he doesn't take a lot of time to enjoy himself. I know he's into sports, but I've never heard him talk about doing any of those things. He's always traveling for work. That's it."

"This could be a particularly busy time for him. You never know."

"You're right. Still, I wouldn't want that sort of fortune if I couldn't enjoy it. What's the point?"

"I'm with you on that," she agrees. "So, I guess you won't be including this in your new book. This icky conflict stuff."

"*Au contraire*. This is gold. This can be what threatens to keep my characters apart. It's practically writing itself."

"At least something good can come out of it, I

guess." She sounds depressed though, which I hate.

"Perk up! This is one book of many. One potential boyfriend of many too." Yes, I'm very positive about this. Entirely in control. I have the whole thing in hand.

So what if I have a sick feeling in my heart? Flowers or no flowers, I don't feel good about what happened last night, and I'm disappointed in myself for wanting more from Blake than he's ready or able to give. I'm not supposed to be catching feelings, as Hayley put it.

"You're trying to smile, but it looks more like a grimace," she sighs. "Maybe you're not cut out to be the casual-dating type of girl. Maybe it was irresponsible of me to talk you into this."

"Or … maybe Blake's somebody I really want to be with, and I wish things would work out," I sigh, swirling what's left of my latte in its cup. "It's bad luck that I found somebody I really, really like on the first try."

"Maybe you'll go out with a creep next time," Hayley suggests.

"The amount of hope in your voice is frightening. Just thought I'd let you know."

Chapter Twenty

ANOTHER SURPRISE DATE.

Not a surprise as in, *Surprise, I showed up at your door.*

Surprise as in, *Surprise, we're going someplace, and I'm not telling you where.*

I like Blake. A lot. And I was thrilled when he called to ask if I was free on Sunday. After spending the week wondering about a follow-up to the millions of flowers he'd sent, after writing my fingers to the bone, hearing from him was like rain in the desert.

With me being the desert. I don't even know if my metaphors make sense anymore. After writing so hard for a solid week, I can barely think straight.

Now, running down the stairs to meet Blake at the car, I have to wonder what he has in mind. He told me to dress casually. *Are we going to Philly for a famous cheesesteak? Or maybe to a movie, like normal people?* I find it hard to imagine him sitting in a movie theater with a hundred others, but who knows? He tries to be a regular person, no matter how far removed he is from regular life.

He's wearing jeans. I didn't even think he owned jeans.

"Hi," he offers, looking a little sheepish. He runs a hand through his sandy-blond hair. *Is he nervous?*

"Hi yourself. You look great."

And he does. I've always been a sucker for jeans and good shoes. Especially if the man in question can wear jeans as well as he can. I need to fan myself at the sight of him. A cold shower might be nice too.

"Thanks. So do you, but then you always do." He must take heart at the way I don't, you know, rip his head off at first sight.

Did he think I was still mad at him? I wouldn't have agreed to go out with him if I were still upset.

His smile is more genuine, and he even leans down to kiss my cheek.

"So, where are we going?" I have to ask when we're in the car. "I can't stand the suspense."

"Sorry about that." He grimaces. "I didn't know if my plans would work out at first, so I thought it made more sense to keep quiet until things firmed up."

"And they have?"

"They have." He rubs his hands on his thighs.

He really is nervous. Why?

"What's wrong? Is this a bad day?"

Goodness knows, things move fast in his world. A sudden phone call, and everything turns upside down.

He shakes his head, frowning. "No, don't get that idea. I'm a little nervous, I admit. I told myself this was totally casual—and it is! Don't get me wrong. It's completely casual, just a simple dinner. No big deal."

"Dinner where?"

It can't be anyplace fancy since he's as dressed down as I've ever seen him. The shirt he's wearing is open at the first two buttons, for heaven's sake. That's pretty casual.

"Dinner ... at my mom's house."

I should've known somehow. I should've sensed it. "Stop playing," I whisper anyway, hoping this is a joke. Because it has to be. He can't be serious. "You're taking me to meet your mother?"

"It's not like that."

"You are taking me. To meet. Your mother. There's not much of a gray area there. You're either introducing me to her or you aren't. That's a big deal."

Darn him. He looks legitimately surprised by my reaction, like it never once occurred to him that I might freak out.

"I'm not bringing you out there as my girlfriend! I told Mom you were an author, and she asked who, and I mentioned your name, and she was more excited than I'd imagined she'd be. I had no idea she'd recognize you."

"Okay ..." I'm not convinced. If anything, knowing I'm meeting her as a fan leaves me shakier than ever. *His mother. His mother! What is wrong with him? Isn't he supposed to be smart? How'd he end up making so much money?*

"Turns out, she's read your books since my sister recommended them. They're both big fans." Then, as an afterthought, "Oh, she'll be there too."

"Your sister?" I squeak. This is entirely too much for my poor, overtaxed heart. It's practically beating out of my chest. "Are you trying to kill me?"

"Come here." He pulls me into his arms, chuckling softly. I could smack him silly for acting like this is funny. "It's not that big a deal. I promise. I thought it would be nice for them and for you. A departure. Something quiet and relaxed."

"Relaxed." I laugh. "Meanwhile, I'm wondering how high my blood pressure can go before I have a stroke."

"We don't have to do this. I should've talked it over with you first." He sounds so sad as he leans back, looking down at me. "That's a real problem of mine. I get a great idea and don't think about how it might be read by others. I'm so sorry."

It seems like he's always having to apologize. Granted, he needs to—this is a truly messed up idea, sneaking me away to his mother's house without finding out if I feel comfortable with the idea—but still. His heart is in the right place.

"It's fine. Really. I'm sure they're both very nice. I was surprised, is all. I mean, you know what taking a girl to meet your mother usually implies."

Was this the right thing to say? I don't know, but it's not like this is the first time I've tripped over my tongue.

His eyes widen. "I don't want you to have that idea," he deadpans without so much as a ghost of a smile or a twinkle in his eye.

"I don't have it. Which is why this came as a surprise. That's what I'm trying to say."

But the damage has been done. He stiffens and sits up straight, his arms loosening when they held me so firmly only a few seconds ago.

This is going well.

The flight is uneventful with Blake holding my hand now and then. When he's not busy on his phone. Here I was, sort of hoping we could get in a little smooching today. But no, he's freaked out because I suggested the obvious conclusion anybody with half a brain would have come to.

"No champagne today," I note with a soft laugh. "That's for the best. I'm not good at first impressions as it is. I don't need alcohol making things worse."

"Stop saying things like that." He finally looks up from the screen, dark eyes locking on to mine. "You're too hard on yourself. You're not the awkward person you think you are."

"Blake, when we first met, I was on my hands and knees with my hair in my face. Pretty awkward."

"Not your fault either. And in case you couldn't tell"—he plants a kiss on my cheek and then another on my lips—"it didn't make me like you any less."

I can't argue with that. We land in Phoenix—where, of course, it's two hours earlier than on the East Coast. *Plenty of time for me to get to know the family before dinner.* My stomach lurches at the thought.

Though if he thinks this is okay, that there's nothing deeper going on, I'm willing to play along. I only hope neither woman asks what I'm currently working on.

"Can I ask a favor?"

We're in a rental car that was waiting for us when we landed, a sleek Maserati that practically floats over the road.

"Of course."

"If either of them asks what I'm working on right now, can you pretend you don't know? I'd rather keep it on the down-low—the content's a little steamier than I usually write."

"Sure thing. You're right; that would be awkward if they knew we'd started seeing each other to provide inspiration." He pats my leg and then squeezes a little. "Hey. You don't have to feel embarrassed by what you're writing. People have sex. I know it's not what you usually write, but I doubt anybody would clutch their pearls too hard at a few sex scenes."

"You might be surprised. I just barely managed to unclench my hand from around my own pearls."

"Am I at least half-decent in this book? At the sex stuff?"

"Blake."

"I wanna know! Can you blame me? Is my character hung?"

"He's not really your character. He's somebody based on you. His apartment looks a lot like yours, and his jet is similar. He has a friend who owns the hottest restaurant in Dallas, and he takes her there on a whim."

"Okay. I can live with those differences." He squeezes my leg again. "But if you could give him a huge cock, that would be nice."

My cheeks just about burst into flames, but I have to laugh as I tell him, "I'll see what I can do."

I don't know what I expected his mother's house to be like. I knew he'd bought it for her, so it had to be nice. Large, comfortable. I didn't expect what looks like an oversize cottage, the white picket fence that surrounds it covered in climbing vines, which also decorate the white brick walls. There's a lush green lawn, cut down the center by a brick pathway leading up to the door and flowering bushes lining either side.

"I didn't expect it to be so green," I admit, looking around in wonder. "It's beautiful."

"Mom's always had a green thumb. She did a lot of research into what grows best out here. I think it helped her adjust—she didn't want to leave home, you know. But it was either move or have constant bronchitis."

He leads me up the pathway, my hand in his, and I wish I had brought a little gift or something.

A blonde bullet comes running at us as soon as the door's open and we're one step inside the massive foyer. "Hi, hi, hi, oh my gosh!" It all comes out at once as a pair of arms close around me.

"Britt! Don't maul her!" But Blake is laughing as he frees me from who I'm guessing is his sister. "Let's not scare her away, okay?"

"It's okay." I hold a hand out to Britt, who's basically a miniature female version of her brother with longer hair and a wider smile. "I'm Kitty."

"I know!" she gushes as she squeezes my hand until it almost hurts. "I'm sorry. I know I'm making a huge fool out of myself, but I've been a fan of yours for so long. When I found out Blake was bringing you for dinner, I just about died. I mean, I literally almost stopped breathing. I love your books so much."

She's a whirlwind, to put it mildly.

"Thank you so much for that." I smile, breathless and shaky and hoping she doesn't mind the new direction my work is going in.

Her smile is just about blinding. "Come on. Let's go find Mom. She's in the kitchen, I guess. Killing the fatted calf and all that."

"No pressure," Blake murmurs in a warning

way as his sister slides an arm around my waist and steers me through the charming, cozy house and into a sunny kitchen.

Mrs. Marlin is a beautiful woman with a warm, loving smile. "There's my fella." She grins as she goes in to hug Blake. Her Philly accent is much stronger than either Britt's or Blake's—his is almost nonexistent really. I guess he must've worked it out of his system over time.

"Hey, Mom. This is Kitty. I was a real idiot and didn't tell her we were coming here until we were on the way to the hangar, so the three of you can berate me all you want." He has a way of defusing any situation, this Blake. No wonder he's so successful in business.

His mother smacks his arm. Britt smacks the other.

"Why would you do that to her?" Britt demands before smacking him again. "You're a real moron."

I can't deny that this is fun to watch. The big, powerful mogul being scolded by the women in his life. He's even red-faced, which is like the cherry on top. It takes a lot of my self-control to keep from laughing.

"Forgive him, honey," his mother sighs before giving me a much gentler hug than her daughter did. "I did my best to raise him right, but I might've dropped him on his head once. The early days are a blur."

I like her even more than I imagined I would.

Chapter Twenty-One

"WHEN BLAKE'S FATHER passed, I was sure I'd fall to pieces." Mrs. Marlin takes a sip of her wine, staring thoughtfully out at the garden she clearly loves and tends for all she's worth. "I did for a little while. At least the kids were old enough that they could take care of themselves—for the most part."

"Nobody could blame you for that, Mrs. Marlin."

"Sara, please." She smiles, glancing my way. "If I can call you Kitty, you can call me by my first name.

"I think it affected Blake harder than Britt. He and his father had had a talk near the end. I know my husband didn't feel he left much behind for us. His plant had closed down when the economy tanked, and he was never the same. I don't think it's a coincidence that Blake became obsessed with wealth after that."

"You think it was all because he'd lost his father?"

"And his father felt like a failure. Yes, I think that played a big part—though, of course, he'd never admit that. And I would never breathe a word of it."

"Neither would I," I whisper. And I won't. But this gives me some much-needed insight into Blake. Now, I understand what drove him to be the best. I can use that for my hero.

Jeez, am I seriously thinking about my book right now? Here I am, accusing Blake of not being able to separate himself from work …

"Thank you for having me here tonight," I murmur, and I mean it with all my heart. I can hear Blake and Britt laughing as they wash dishes inside, teasing the way brothers and sisters do. He sounds younger here, happier. "It's so beautiful. I love hearing Blake laugh so much too."

"So do I. It's been a long time since he found a girl worthy of bringing home."

Ouch. No pressure or anything.

"He even left his phone out here," Sara notices, nodding to where the device sits on the table in front of us.

"Wow. That never happens," I marvel.

"I know. The fact that he's able to do that after taking the time out to bring you here gives me hope."

"Sara …"

"Don't worry." She smiles; she's wise in the way only a mother can be. "I'm not dreaming about grandchildren just yet. Though it would be nice. But he can't be an easy man to date. I give you credit."

Ouch again. Is this a trap? I guess she's not the sort of person to lay traps—though who knows?

"He's very busy. I wish he'd take more time for himself. Not for me. For him."

"I'm hoping he'll start doing more of that now that the two of you are seeing each other," she muses, swirling the wine in her glass.

I don't have the heart to tell her he's already blown me off more than once.

It's like the stinking phone knows we were talking about it because it rings a moment later.

"Blake!" I say, my heart sinking as I reach for it. "Your phone's ringing!"

"My hands are soaked," he calls out through the half-open window. "Can you grab it?"

"Wow," I whisper, eyes wide. Sara chuckles as I answer, "Hello? Blake Marlin's phone."

A silent pause.

"Who's this?" says a woman's voice.

"This is a friend of Blake's. He's on his way to the phone right now."

Another pause.

"Kitty? Is this Kitty?" The way she says my name, it might as well be obscene.

"It is." I exchange a look with Sara, who shrugs. "But not for much longer. He's on his way."

"Where is he? Where are you? He's been un-reachable for most of the day, and I've spent my entire Sunday trying to put out a fire for him. Would you like to take over the job of being his assistant? Because honestly, I don't know how much longer I can take this."

"I ... don't feel comfortable with this conversation," I announce, my hand tightening around the phone. "This isn't any of my business."

"But it is because he's been a basket case since the two of you met at that conference. I was there. I saw it happen."

Right. This is the girl who reminded Blake of his schedule while he was helping me. She struck me as harried and irritated. I can imagine why.

But still.

"I don't make decisions for him," I remind her. "He does that on his own. If you have a problem with the way he's been lately, he's the one to take that up with. Not me."

"What's going on?" Blake's by my side now, frowning deeply. "Who is that?"

"Give him the phone," the girl snaps.

I give him the phone before turning away, trembling. "I don't like conflict, especially with people I don't know," I whisper to Sara, who pats my shoulder.

"That was uncalled for," she murmurs. "I think he heard enough of it to know what was going on. That girl won't have a job for long."

"It's my fault."

"It's not. She shouldn't have thrown her problems at you like that. If Blake doesn't fire her, I'll be disappointed in him." She turns her head toward

Blake, who's walking the length of the garden and barking instructions into the phone. "Something tells me the night just came to an end."

"I'm awfully sorry." And I am. This has been really nice, much nicer than I imagined when I found out where we were going.

"So am I, sweetie." She stands when Blake approaches us. "Leaving so soon?"

"How did you know?" His shoulders are around his ears, his hands clenched in fists. "Sorry for the sudden departure."

"I've heard that before." She sounds so sad, almost as sad as I feel for all of us.

It's not until we're on the jet that I even dare to ask what happened—asking while he drove us to the jet didn't seem like a hot idea. "Is there a problem I need to know about? Because your assistant seemed really mad at me."

"She's not my assistant anymore. I have to train a new one. Just one more thing to do." He leans back in his seat with a sigh. "I need a drink."

"I'll fix you one," I offer, eyeing the drink cart.

"No, that's okay. You're not my employee. I thought tonight was going so well before that happened too."

"So did I. It was going well. I love your mom and Britt. They're great."

"They loved you too. I knew they would." Though he's not smiling. He's only speaking the words. He's not feeling them right now.

"Is there something big going on? With your business, I mean. Is that why she was so upset that she couldn't reach you?"

"There's always something big going on. You should be used to that by now."

"Um, I am—somewhat." Here we go again, with him being in a bad mood and taking it out on me. "We don't have to talk about it."

"I don't want to."

"But you realize you can't keep me closed out forever—me or anybody else you're dating. You know that, right? Because no matter how much you want to keep your work and personal life separate, it'll never happen when work is such a huge part of your life."

"Enough, okay? I don't need this from you right now."

"Excuse me?" I ask, sitting up straighter. My ears practically perk up, like an animal sensing a challenge. "I didn't do anything to earn this. I'm worried about you, is all, and it annoys me when I see things getting to you this way."

"Annoys you?" he asks, arching one eyebrow.

"For your sake," I sigh, rolling my eyes. "Because you were actually happy for a little while there, and now, you're miserable all over again. Angry. Your shoulders are up here." I hunch them up to mimic the way his currently sit. "You were laughing with Britt just a minute before you took the phone. It was beautiful. Now? You're a mess."

"Please, keep heaping it on me," he groans. "Make me feel worse. Add to my stress."

"You're right. I'm not allowed to care. I'm supposed to walk around with my mouth hanging open, amazed at how wonderful your life is. I'm not supposed to have an opinion, and I'm definitely not supposed to care anything about you." I charge out of my seat and wish like heck I could leave the plane, but of course, that's not an option.

Instead, I settle for slamming myself into a seat across from Blake, folding my arms and swinging one leg back and forth after crossing it over the other. He spends the rest of the flight making terse phone calls. I might as well not be here.

How does this keep happening?

How many clues do I need dropped in my lap before I figure out that this is never going to work?

Chapter Twenty-Two

"I'D GIVE IT all up for you, right this minute," Bryan murmured, tucking a strand of hair behind Phoebe's ear before sliding his hand around to the back of her head. "None of it matters without you."

She couldn't believe her ears. It was almost too much to believe. Was this a dream? She'd imagined this moment so many times after all. Odds were, she was asleep.

"What are you doing?" he asked, laughing gently when she squeezed her eyes shut and then opened them wide.

She did it again instead of answering right away, but the result was the same. "This is how I wake myself up from a dream when I know I'm dreaming," she explained with a sheepish smile.

"You think this is a dream?" he asked.

"I hope it isn't—but if it is, it's the best dream I've ever had. It's a miracle."

"No. You're the miracle," he whispered, pulling her in. "I'm only the lucky guy who gets to have you in his life. I know I don't deserve you. But I'll spend the rest of my life doing everything I can to earn you, Phoebe. So long as you'll let me."

"I'll let you," she promised, throwing her arms around his neck a moment before the tears started flowing. "Always. I love you so much."

"And I love you." He smiled before brushing his lips against hers in the softest, sweetest kiss, one more tender than he'd ever given her before.

But that didn't last long because he was soon devouring her mouth, plunging his tongue inside and plundering her, hungry and determined to claim her once and for all.

And she wanted him to. Needed him to. He guided her to the desk, and she leaned against it. She was already halfway to unbuttoning his shirt by the time he worked the skirt up over her hips. She had to have him, all of him, had to lose herself in him while he did the same with her.

I have to take a break, pushing away from the laptop with tears in my eyes. Phoebe's supposed to be the one crying, not me.

She's also supposed to be finding the love of her life and preparing for a hot, raunchy but ultimately tender and loving sex session on her boss/boyfriend's desk. That's most certainly not my situation.

I wish I could stop thinking about Blake, imagining him as being the one loving me—or rather, Phoebe. It's all too messy. I should never have started this. Now that things have fallen apart and it's obvious that Blake could never be anybody's boyfriend until he gets his business worked out. This was a terrible idea.

If I had a little closure with him, that would be one thing. But ten days of radio silence on his end after I've texted and even left voice mails, the message has finally come through.

He's done with me. I guess that's for the best.

And if I don't get this book over to Maggie in the next week, at the very most, she'll be done with me too. Nothing like a whole lot of pressure to make the creative juices dry up until they're nonexistent, right?

The sudden knock at the door as I'm coming back from washing my tearstained face makes me jump. It could only be Matt. People don't normally visit out of nowhere. Even Hayley knows better than to do that.

It's only when the aroma of steak and onions reaches my nose before I've opened the door that I realize there's one person who doesn't know better. And even if he did, he wouldn't care. I mean, he flew me to his mother's house without clearing with me whether or not I actually wanted to go.

Showing up at my apartment unannounced is, like, nothing compared to that.

Blake looks like a million bucks, as always, wearing one of his tailored suits. Meanwhile, I haven't washed my hair in three days.

My greasy hair isn't nearly as interesting as the greasy paper bag that Blake holds up for my inspection, however. I mean, the entire hall smells like a sandwich shop. A delicious, mouthwatering sandwich shop.

"I don't know who to say hello to first," I admit while wishing like heck I were wearing something better suited for a moment like this. Something a little nicer than a sweatshirt and yoga pants from this morning's workout.

What can I say? I'm proud that I even managed to get a workout in. Showering and getting dressed afterward was beyond the realm of my powers.

"The sandwiches, of course." Blake smirks. "I flew them straight in from Philly just a little while ago, packed in one of those foil-lined bags that keeps the heat in."

"You could've saved a lot of trouble, you know. A simple phone call would've done the trick." But I step aside anyway. "Come on in. Sorry for the mess. I'm on a deadline."

He sighs as he steps inside. "I can't seem to get it right with you, can I?"

"I'm not trying to make you feel bad—but maybe, just maybe, call a girl when she's trying to get in touch with you, so she doesn't think you died." We go to the kitchen, where he lays the sandwiches on the counter. "Can I get you something to drink?"

What are we doing? I feel like we're playing parts in a script, like we're saying words and going through motions that don't fit the situation.

"Water, please. I'm dehydrated from the flight."

"Let me guess. You've been on the road all week?"

"Actually, yes." He shrugs, accepting a bottle of water from the fridge. "Philly was a pitstop on the way up from Atlanta."

"Do you ever stop?"

"Not really." He unwraps one long sandwich and then the other. "I should've asked if you were hungry."

"Even if I wasn't, I'd climb over your dead body to get my hands on this," I confess. "Don't forget. I'm on a deadline. Things like eating tend to fall by the wayside."

And, oh boy, is it a good sandwich. Rich, meaty, cheesy, speckled with sweet caramelized onions and fried mushrooms. I could just about melt into the floor. "My gosh," I manage to say before taking another bite.

"Not quite the same as having one on-site, but I figured a little extra time wouldn't make that much of a difference." He takes a bite, groaning. "I was right."

"You were right."

We exchange a long look, food forgotten for a moment.

"But just about the sandwiches though," he murmurs before wiping his mouth on a napkin. "I was wrong about a lot of things. I was wrong, period. I'm wrong."

"You're not wrong," I whisper, shaking my head.

He's sitting on the other side of the counter,

facing me, but we might as well be a million miles from each other. That granite countertop is a cavern between us.

His dark eyes are dull, without that spark of light I first noticed in them when we met. "What's the problem then? Why can't I get it right? I've found a beautiful, amazing girl who makes me laugh and drives me crazy, but I can't make it work with you. I've never wanted to make it work so much. Not ever. But it seems like I'm not cut out for life with a perfect woman."

"I'm not perfect."

"You are, for me—at least, on paper." He takes another bite, though this one doesn't have the gusto the first bite did.

I wait as he chews and sense he's stalling for time, trying to get his thoughts together.

I finally jump in because it's breaking my heart to hear him talk this way. "You're not wrong. You're the best, really. I would love to make this work too. But the life you lead doesn't mesh with a relationship. Not because you aren't cut out for it, but because you have to make a few changes. Not that ambition is bad. It's great. You've done incredible things."

"What difference does it make if I can't have the person I want?"

I have to duck my head to hide the tears threatening to flow. It's my turn to take a huge bite, just to have the excuse to stop talking for a while.

He fills in the silence for me. "I know I have a lot of work to do. I guess I should thank you for that. I wouldn't have thought about it until you put it right in front of my face. I need big gestures like that before something gets through my thick skull."

"I had a feeling." I snicker. "I mean, you're the guy who flew me out to meet his mom with no warning whatsoever."

"I'll never live that one down."

"Nor should you." I point to his steak. "Eat. You look worn out."

"Yes, ma'am."

"So, have you found a new assistant yet?" I ask. I have to. I can't help it. That little brat yelled at me—or practically.

He nods. "Yeah, there are two of them actually. At the suggestion of a few colleagues."

"Get out. Two assistants?"

"Yep. They work together, handling different parts of my schedule. It was unfair to put all of that on one person for so long. Now, I might work a little more efficiently." He winks. "Progress. One step at a time."

"I'm proud of you." And I am.

I only wish those steps had happened a long time ago. He might have been ready for me by now if that were the case.

No. That's not right. Everything happens for a reason, and there's a reason things worked out the way they did. He didn't fail. Neither did I. It's just not right for us.

I don't have to like it, but that's the truth.

We make small talk for a while after that. He compliments the apartment and admires the view of the park while I scan the rooms for hints of anything too embarrassing.

Before long though, it's time for him to go. I want so much for him to stay, and I sense he wants the same thing. But that would be a mistake.

Instead of inviting him to bed, I walk him to the door, and we kiss just once more before hugging. It's a nice kiss, gentle, and we both taste like steak and onions, so it's not terribly romantic or sexy.

Probably for the best, all things considered.

"Thank you for everything," I whisper, standing on my tiptoes so I can reach his ear. "Thank you so much."

"Thank you, Kathryn Antoinette," he whispers back, squeezing tight. "You've given me a lot more than I gave you. If you could give me one more thing ..."

I lean back, looking up into his eyes. "What's that?"

A smile plays over his mouth, making his lips twitch. "Please, make sure my character is well hung. Nobody else will know he's a stand-in for me, but I will."

"I'll see what I can do," I say, already knowing he will be.

Chapter Twenty-Three

HAS MAGGIE GOTTEN back to you yet?

My heart sinks when I find a text from Hayley, which is different since I usually love it when she texts. But she's not the person I've spent the last five days waiting for word from. She's not the person who has me pacing the floor and rearranging the books and scrubbing the grout in the bathroom.

Grout-scrubbing is truly the bottom of the barrel when it comes to finding ways to distract myself. That and, like, cleaning the oven. But I don't use the oven that much, so ...

No, I type back. *You'll be the first to know, I promise.*

What the heck is taking Maggie so long?, she replies.

I roll my eyes. *Yeah, I've been asking myself the same question. Maybe she's preparing a speech to let me down gently,* I suggest with a bunch of throw-up face emojis.

Not a chance. And if she wanted to let you go, she'd just drop you, Hayley texts back, trying to be encouraging.

Somehow, that doesn't make me feel much better, I reply. *I'll let you know.*

I then toss the phone aside because I can't even stand to hold it in my hand. I'm too jittery. It's a good thing I don't have an appetite since I'd probably upchuck anything I tried to eat.

It's clear Maggie has no idea what it's like, being in this position. With her career on the line. Not just a career either. My book is something that came out of my head, completely mine. My thoughts. Heck, even my experiences, to a degree.

There's nothing as harrowing as handing something that came from you off to somebody else and then waiting for their judgment. I might as well have handed off my heart.

Though my heart's a little sore right now, even a week after ending things with Blake. I should be grateful that I had the opportunity to date somebody like him—and not because he's a billionaire.

Because he's wonderful. Because he has so much to offer. I only wish it were me he was offering it to.

I've only asked myself, oh, three hundred times this week whether I made the biggest mistake of my life when I ended our strange, sporadic relationship. If I should've held out longer. If I was too demanding, if I expected too much.

It's easy to think things like that in weak moments. When I'm feeling more clearheaded, like after a walk in the park or after doing my yoga practice in the morning, I know I did the right thing for me by agreeing that there couldn't be a future for us as things currently stood. Blake is amazing and sexy and sweet, and if he got his personal life figured out, I'd be glad to take another chance at us being together.

But that's not the way things are right now, and I don't know if I want to wait for what could be years until he finds balance and comes to terms with his success.

The phone rings. I trip as I throw myself across the room and land face-first on the sofa while still scrambling to reach the stupid thing.

"Oh jeez. Oh jeez."

It's Maggie.

Now that she's calling, I wish she hadn't. *Was I seriously hoping for this moment to arrive? What the heck is wrong with me? Have I been a masochist all along, and I'm only now just finding out?*

"Hello?" I whisper on answering, pushing myself up into a sitting position. *Please, please, don't let her fire me for good. Please, let her tell me we can work with what I gave her.*

Nobody wants to hear their writing needs a lot of work, but that's still better than having it rejected full-out.

"Kitty. Antoinette. Valentine."

I squeeze my eyes just as tightly shut as I can. "Does that mean this is a good phone call?" *Please, please, please let this be a good phone call.*

"Where have you been hiding this filthy mind of yours for so long?" Maggie asks with all the pride of a mom putting one of those *My Kid's an Honor*

Student bumper stickers on the back of her minivan. It's a little weird, frankly.

My eyes slowly open as hope sparks in my chest. "Uh, I don't know. I guess I didn't know it was there in the first place."

"Well"—she laughs—"don't lose it. Because this is gold. We can pretty much print money once this is published. And your readers are going to be thirsty for the next one and the one after that …"

"So, you like it?"

"Like it? I love it! Oh, when he fingers her in the car? I could barely breathe the entire scene, waiting for somebody to come up and open the door on them. It was so exciting!"

"Yeah," I whisper. "It was pretty exciting."

She doesn't need to know just how true to life that scene was—and now that she's brought up the idea of somebody opening the door, I'm super glad that never occurred to me at the moment. Talk about a mood killer.

"And when they first did it on the jet? Please tell me that actually happened."

"Uh, Maggie"—I chuckle—"this is getting a little personal."

"You're right; you're right. I'm sorry. I'm just so thrilled at how hot the book is. I didn't want to have to part ways with you. It was keeping me up at night, the thought of having to let you go. I think this is a great new direction for you. You can only get more popular after this."

"I hope you're right." My fingers are certainly crossed.

"So, what's your plan for the next book? Typical advance—though I'm sure that'll change as this new brand takes off." She's so confident; it's almost enough to make me feel the same.

Almost.

"Let's take a minute to breathe, please," I beg with a hollow laugh. "My brain is basically mush right now."

"You'd better un-mush it soon, young lady." Yes, there's the Maggie I know and only somewhat enjoy. She likes me again, which means we can be friends and she can pretend to chide me. "Readers are used to books cranking out a lot faster nowadays."

There's nothing to do but bite my tongue and pray it doesn't fall off. "Sure. I get it." Just like I get that she thinks I can go from one man to another the way I change underwear. I don't know if that's an insult or what.

"Take a few days," she offers, generous as always. "Once you've decided who you're dating next, let me know. I might be able to get a cover worked out in advance this time, knowing which trope you're writing."

"Got it."

"Keep it filthy."

"Will do," I sigh.

"Maybe a threesome this time?"

"Maggie."

"Okay, okay. Just a suggestion. Don't knock it 'til you try it."

"Maggie!" I gasp.

I can imagine her sitting at her desk, the city laid out behind her, laughing merrily.

"I'm just saying. You don't know whether or not you'll like something until you try it."

I'm going to pretend she's not speaking from experience—and that she wasn't imagining me and some guy having sex throughout the book, which is a thought so icky that I don't know what to do with it.

"Okay. I'll keep an open mind."

I most certainly will not.

Though who knows? I didn't think I could manage to write something half as graphic as I did. There's a whole world out there I haven't come anywhere close to experiencing.

But a threesome? Maybe I can imagine one and just pretend I went through it for real.

The second we're off the phone, I do a little victory dance across the apartment, pumping my fists. "Yes! Yes, yes!"

It occurs to me after I work myself up into a sweaty mess that there's somebody I should be thanking for real. If it wasn't for Blake, there wouldn't be any book at all. We haven't spoken in a week, and I'm running the risk of tangling with his new assistant, but I figure, calling his cell and leaving a short message can't hurt.

"Hi. I was hoping you'd call, so I wouldn't have to get up the courage to call you."

I should have known better than to think he'd let it go to voice mail.

Gosh, I've missed his voice. The little touch of humor in it is so him too.

"Then, you're lucky I got good news today since that's why I'm calling." Then, it occurs to me. "But if you're busy, I won't keep you."

"I'm not, if you can believe that. I decided to take a little time off and lick my wounds. I'm at my mom's house."

"No kidding! How is she?"

"When she's not smacking me upside the head for letting you get away? She's great."

I know he's kidding—mostly—but my heart sinks anyway. "Blake …"

"I'm not trying to make you feel bad, I swear. You were right. I need to find a way to sort my life out. I can't keep up the pace I'm working at now. I don't wanna be the guy who dies, feeling like he didn't leave a legacy, but I don't wanna be on my deathbed, wondering when life passed me by either."

"I'm really glad to hear that," I murmur. It's getting dark out now, the city coming to life the way only New York can at this time of day. "You deserve it. You're such a great person, and you deserve to be happy."

"What about you?"

"What about me?"

"Do you feel comfortable with what you wrote? Does that make you happy?"

"Oof. With the difficult questions and everything."

That warm laughter of his. It's so nice.

"I mean it. What do you think?"

"Well, that's the good-news part. My editor adores the book, and I have you to thank for that as much as anybody else. It turned out well. Even I like it, which is saying something. I never like my finished product when I first read it."

"That's great, and I'm glad for you, but that's not what I asked. How did you feel about writing it? Does the final product make you happy?"

Does it? I wish there were an easy answer. "I mean, once I got into it, it wasn't nearly as difficult as I'd thought. I was being stubborn. A little snobby too. If readers are as voracious when it comes to this writing as my editor makes it sound, there's gotta be value in it. And the readers are what matter. I'm doing this for them, not for my ego or my bank account. I guess I lost sight of that. Maybe I never had sight of it in the first place."

"You live a charmed life," he gently points out. "We all need a challenge now and then, something to shake up the way we see things."

"This was definitely a challenge. I think I could get used to writing dirtier romance. Though honestly, you made it easier."

"Tell me you didn't get too specific, please."

"You can read it!"

"Tell me."

"I mean ... I changed some circumstances," I squeak, squeezing my eyes shut again.

"If you tell me all you left out was that burp you laid down—"

"Blake!"

"Is it?"

"No! I mean, yes, I left that out. But no. I changed a bunch of things. Jeez."

"Okay. I'll take your word for it. But if my sister throws her copy in my face and accuses me of being a pervert, you'll be hearing from me."

"I hope I hear from you regardless," I murmur, leaning against the window frame.

"You will, for sure," he promises before saying good-bye.

It doesn't seem like we said everything left to be said, but I don't know if it would be possible to do that. There's too much in my heart.

I really hope the next person I date doesn't have me falling. There's no way I could handle this again.

"Hayley?" I ask when she answers. Sure, I told her I'd call her first, but I think she'll understand. "Could you spare an hour or two tonight?"

"Oh, sweetheart," she groans. "I'm so sorry. I made sure my schedule was clear tonight, just in case."

"Wait. What?"

"What?"

"That's the faith you had in me, huh?"

"You sounded sad!" She laughs. "What was I supposed to think? So, you got the green light? You're getting published?"

Maybe I was sad, just a little, thinking about Blake. But it's time to start moving on, and tonight's as good a place to start as any. "We're going out. My treat. Look hot."

Chapter Twenty-Four

THE SUN IS on its way down by the time the door across the hall opens and closes. It's probably stalkery of me, but I can't help listening to see whether Matt goes down the stairs or up to the roof. When I don't hear him jogging down to the street, I know he's gone up to enjoy the sunset.

Which is my cue.

I haven't said a word to him since suggesting he drop dead a few weeks ago. It probably shouldn't bother me so much—this silence between us. We went a whole year without talking before that fateful day in the hall after I raided the liquor store.

This silence is different. This is the sort of silence that comes from one person telling the other one to drop dead. Not my proudest moment, not by a long shot.

By the time I get up there, six-pack in hand, he's setting up his folding chair. His glance my way earns me a smirk.

"I notice you have a chair up here now too," he murmurs, positioning himself.

"It was a good idea." I shrug, going to where my

chair is tucked away. "Though it could've been anyone's chair. It didn't have to be mine."

"Something told me the chair with unicorns and rainbows painted on the seat belonged to the girl across the hall. Call me psychic." He watches me set up my chair with a bemused expression. "I guess I can't expect a little peace and quiet up here ever again, can I?"

"We don't have to talk. Look, I'll take my chair and my icy-cold beer over here."

I pick up the chair and start across the roof, but Matt shakes his head.

"No, not when beer is involved. You plan on sharing?"

"I brought it up to share. Consider it an olive branch." I hand him the entire pack and accept one of the cans he pulls from the container. "Thanks."

"I should be thanking you." Yet he doesn't.

I don't expect him to either. I know him too well by now.

"And I've been wanting to say something too," I croak. *Why is this so hard?* "I, um … you know … I shouldn't have …"

"Don't worry about it." He grins. "No harm done. I was being a dick. I think we're even now."

What a relief. Conflict has always been easier for me on the page than it is in real life.

Plopping down in the chair, I crack open the can with a sigh. "Welp, my first smutty book is finished. My editor doesn't think it'll need much work, and there's already a cover in mind for it. I guess this new phase in my career is a success. So far."

"So far?" He snickers. "What, you have doubts?"

"How can I not? I'm always going to wonder whether I have what it takes, no matter how impressed my editor seems with the new book." The beer doesn't help ease my nerves, though it does bring a smile to my face. "This is good. I'm not usually a beer drinker."

"Why did you buy it then?"

"I thought you might like it."

"Aww." He grins. "You bought beer with me in mind. I'm flattered."

I regret this already. "Don't let it go to your head."

"Too late. I'll be checking all the trees on this block to see which one you carved our initials into."

I have to laugh. It's better to be friends than enemies after all.

He gets serious quickly though, his brows meeting over the bridge of his nose. "I hate to tell you this, Kitty, but you're not the only person in the world who's ever had to question whether they're right for their job. Whether they have what it takes. You know what I mean. Maybe you were past due for a reality check. No offense."

Right. None taken or something. "So, what? You ask yourself if you have what it takes to do a good job?"

His eyes widen. "Duh. Yes. I do. All the time."

"You're serious?"

"Why would I lie? What, do you think I'm just trying to make you feel better?"

"Gee, why would I think that?" I mutter as he laughs like he just heard the funniest thing ever. "It's like I gave you credit for being a decent person for half a second. I should have known better."

"Come on," he chides, still chuckling. "I was trying to have, you know, a sharing moment with you. Like, yeah, I can be vulnerable. I have feelings." He bats his eyelashes, touching a hand to his chest.

"Okay, you were being serious. So, you feel shaky at your job sometimes? You wonder if you're cut out for it?"

"At least once a week," he admits, examining his can like it holds the secrets of the universe. "It's one of those things. The market fluctuates more than usual, and when it gets overwhelming, I wonder if I'm doing the right thing. I mean, I'm investing somebody else's money. I have a big responsibility. Why do you think I'm up so early in the morning?"

"Because you're a freak who likes getting up early in the morning?"

"I don't like it that much."

"But you admit, you're a freak."

"Oh, no doubt." He winks. "I'm up because I have to review my performance and adjust as needed. It's stressful as hell sometimes. I think,

What if I make a mistake? What if I end up losing a ton of money for my client? It's not all fun and games and working from home."

"The way people think my job is," I muse, examining my can this time. "Like it's so easy and romantic. Nothing could be further from the truth most of the time. When I'm on a deadline, I'm lucky if I remember to eat. Sometimes when I'm not even on a deadline."

"Nobody has it easy." He shrugs. "They'd call it play if it wasn't work. But we're both lucky to do what we do, where we do it. I remind myself of that all the time."

"Me too," I agree, nodding.

He's looking at me from the corner of his eye. I can see it. "So … how'd it go with the flower guy? You two still dating now that the book is finished?"

"No, but it doesn't have anything to do with the book. We aren't a good fit."

"It happens."

My shoulders hunch up around my ears. "I know."

"You're upset about it though. I'm sorry."

"I'm a little sad," I admit. "But not upset. Like you said, it happens."

"At least you got to see what it was like to be super rich, right?"

That earns him a laugh. "Yeah, and I know for sure that I'd never want to be that wealthy."

"Liar."

"No! It's true! I couldn't handle it. Always under a microscope, feeling like I have something to prove. There's no end to it either. Like running in a hamster wheel and never getting anywhere."

He mulls this over in silence, staring out at the sunset. "I know this is gonna sound snarky, but there's a reason you're a writer. You have a way of putting things."

That's probably as glowing a compliment I'll ever get from him, so I accept it without a retort. "Thanks."

"So"—his smile is wide, knowing—"what's next? You dated your billionaire boss. Will you try a subway busker next?"

"Hush."

"Trash collector?"

"What would be so bad about that?"

He can't help but smirk, looking me up and down. "Could you make a hot romance out of dating a garbage collector?"

"I could make a hot romance out of dating anybody."

"Ooh. Confident. I like that." He cracks open another beer and then gestures to the rest with his brows lifted.

"Nah. We don't need to tempt fate. You've already seen what happens when I drink too much."

Though, if anything, that hideously embarrassing night broke down the walls that might have otherwise existed between us. I don't have to be cool with him or distant or anything, and I don't find his hotness intimidating now that I've smelled his morning breath.

"True story. I still need to replace my rug."

"I'd be happy to do that for you."

"Eh. Maybe I like having something to hold over your head. Check in with me some other time."

"Anyway, like I was saying, I can write a hot story about any character—though I think my editor wants, you know, standard tropes. Cowboys and firefighters and bad guys."

"Boring."

"You should read my latest book when it comes out and see if you think it's so boring," I suggest. "Better yet, I could give you an advance copy when I get them."

I've seen him look uncomfortable—the whole puking thing and whatnot—but this is a whole other level.

"Oh. Um … I …"

"It would mean a lot to me," I murmur, eyes wide. "I trust your opinion so much."

His mouth falls open in surprise—until he realizes I'm making fun. "Hilarious. Is there comedy in your books too? Because you're so funny."

"Seriously though, no pressure. I'd like to hear your opinion."

"Feeling particularly masochistic today?"

"Nah. I think you'll like it. I do!" I insist when he shoots me a skeptical look. "You could at least try. And then maybe I'll watch you work some-time."

"I don't know who that would be less fun for."

"Fine, fine. Whatever." I take another sip of my beer and turn my face toward the setting sun. The last few streaks of pure gold are starting to fade. It's so beautiful that there's nothing to do but sigh. "It's a shame things like this go away. The sunset, I mean. I wish I could freeze the sky just like that."

"If you could though, would you appreciate it half as much as you do now?"

"Good point."

He sighs too. "Fine. I'll read your book. I hope it's not too raunchy. I don't like that dirty stuff."

I'm too pleased to make a nasty comment. I mean, the sounds coming from his apartment alone are practically enough to fuel my dirty writing.

"Oh, don't worry. I won't offend you."

"Though, I have to say, if there's any marching band music involved, hard pass."

I can't help but giggle. "No marching band mu-sic."

"Nice touch, by the way." He lifts his beer, nod-ding.

"I thought so."

"Don't think I'm not cooking up a way to get back at you for that," he warns.

I lift my beer, too, leaning over to touch my can to his. "I'd be disappointed if you weren't."

ABOUT THE AUTHOR

Jillian Dodd is the *USA Today* best-selling author of more than thirty novels.

She writes fun romances with characters her readers fall in love with—from the boy next door in the *That Boy* trilogy to the daughter of a famous actress in *The Keatyn Chronicles* to a spy who might save the world in the *Spy Girl* series.

She adores writing big fat happily ever afters, wears a lot of pink, buys too many shoes, loves to travel, and is a distracted by anything covered in glitter.